CHASING MAGIC

CHASING MAGIC

HAND OF JUSTICE™ BOOK TWO

JACE MITCHELL

MICHAEL ANDERLE

THE CHASING MAGIC TEAM

Thanks to our Beta Readers
Larry Omans
Chrisa Changala
Mary Morris

Thanks to our JIT Readers

Misty Roa
Diane L. Smith
Angel LaVey
Peter Manis
Paul Westman

Editor

SkyHunter Editing Team

To my best friend, Tucker.

--Jace

*To Family, Friends and
Those Who Love
to Read.
May We All Enjoy Grace
to Live the Life We Are
Called.*

— Michael

"Need more time." Worth was standing behind Riley as he spoke, both of them staring at the docked ship. "You not ready."

Riley heard the desert magician, but she was quiet. She knew what he thought. She'd known for the past two days. The group had been preparing to venture out on the ocean, but New Perthians were mostly a land people. The ships were used by fisherman for food, but no one in New Perth had ever tried venturing beyond their continent.

Riley's new sword, the one Worth had created for her, hung sheathed at her side.

William, the kingdom's other Right Hand, stood to her left.

Riley and William were something akin to knights, although each had a different master. William was under the Prefect, Goland Ire, who was New Perth's ruler. Riley served Goland's son, the Assistant Prefect, Mason Ire.

This small group was now looking at this ship because

of Mason, or rather, because of the mage who had stolen him.

"He powerful. He deep magic. You need time to learn." Worth was adamant about them waiting. He hadn't stopped saying the same thing over and over…

"Give it a fuckin' rest, Worth." William didn't turn around, although there was a slight undercurrent of anger in his voice. He'd been tolerant of the bald warrior mage (as Riley was coming to think of Worth; the man was ridiculously powerful), but Worth's insistence was obviously wearing on William.

"You no remember? You no remember what he did?"

Riley's right hand turned into a fist because *she* did remember. The mage's name was Rendal Hemmons, and Riley had managed to attack him twice—but each time her brilliant speed and skill had easily been thwarted. Tossed aside by the mage's god-like powers. It'd only been a week ago, and the pain was still real for Riley. The pain of losing Mason.

She knew Worth felt the pain too. Worth ruled what New Perth referred to as a "tent city." The name pretty much described it—a city in the middle of a desert that used tents for shelter. Worth had brought ten of his people to help New Perth, and five died at Rendal Hemmons' hands.

William might be grumpy, but Riley understood Worth's concern. She knew his pain was real.

"There's no time to wait, Worth," she whispered. "I wish I could. I wish I could learn what you want to teach me, but Rendal might not wait. He might be hurting Mason right now."

"Aye, we go die then."

She listened as Worth turned from the docks and walked away, his heavy footfalls shaking the wood beneath her.

"Fuck 'em." William shook his head. "I got my fire, and you got… Well, you ain't got no magic, but that's just because I'm better than you. You got your sword, though, and that'll work."

"I can beat you any day of the week and twice on Sunday."

The crew on the ship were nearly ready. Goland's top general, Verith, was double-checking everything now. He was bringing the entire Royal Guard, a group of fifty elite soldiers, and another fifty regular troops. They would have one hundred men, two Right Hands, and although Worth had walked off, he'd be back.

Worth was bringing ten more mages.

Despite Worth's misgivings, Riley thought it was a sizable crew. Plus, the ship was New Perth's best. They weren't a conquering people, but the ship before them would be a match for pirates.

Worth was wrong.

He had to be, because they didn't have time to wait.

"Aye, girl, is this what we'll be travelin' in?"

Riley whipped around, although she didn't reach for her sword. She knew who stood behind her.

William spoke before she even had a chance. "Hell, no! *Hell*, no! You ain't comin', you hear me? You ain't comin', Lucie! Not this time. No way. Prefect Goland didn't clear it."

Lucie stood in front of them; she must have used magic

to keep from being heard. For years, Lucie had shoved her magic down because New Perth had outlawed it. Magic was too dangerous. Times were changing, though, and she'd been more open about what she could do since returning.

From Rendal Hemmons.

From the Dark Mage.

"Ya big dumb animal, Rendal kidnapped me while you ran back here and passed out for three days, 'less you don't remember that?"

Riley smiled.

Lucie wasn't lying.

Rendal *had* kidnapped her, and in the end, had nearly killed her.

"Ya ain't comin', Lucie. We don't have time to watch out for you. We're on a rescue mission, 'less *you* don't remember that?"

"Child, I've forgotten more than you'll ever know. This ain't a discussion, and my 'pologies if you thought it were. I'm goin', and if you don't like it, hike your ass back up to the Prefect and see what he tells ya. I can save ya the time, though, because you'll just be walkin' back here like the punished puppy you are. I spoke with Goland this mornin'."

"You're lyin'," William claimed loudly, but everyone on the dock knew that wasn't true.

Lucie didn't lie.

"Go on and see then. I'll wait," she told him.

William shook his head and turned his back to the older woman.

Riley looked at her.

"Worth is right, ya know," Lucie observed.

"We *don't* have time," Riley replied.

"And that's why I'm comin'," the old woman continued. "Because you're right, too. You'll need as many mages on that ship as it'll hold if you want to stop Rendal, and it'll take us a few days yet to find him. We can work with ya, Worth and I. We can teach you more before we get there. Aye, I'll even work with that big dumb animal who just turned his back on me if he wants."

"You ain't got nothin' to teach me," William grumbled, but Riley had heard the underlying eagerness in his voice. Before the last battle with Rendal, Worth had taught William how to use a bit of magic—enough to light his sword on fire—and William was beyond eager to learn more. He understood how much deadlier it would make him as the Prefect's Right Hand.

"I got more magic in my little finger than you got in your whole body." Lucie turned her focus back to Riley. "We ready?"

"I think so. Worth went to get the tent people, and then we're all loading on. Verith has his troops on board already. We're just waiting for the go-ahead."

"Aye, that works fine, then." She glanced at Riley's hip. "I heard 'bout this sword. Damn blacksmith hasn't stopped talkin' bout it since the tent man made it. Can I take a look?"

Riley didn't hand her sword to anyone ever, neither the one she'd carried for years and lost in the battle with Rendal nor this new one. To Riley, a sword was like a soul. You didn't just hand yours to people. You didn't sell it. Your soul was yours, and a swordsman knew that.

Yet, she knew why Lucie wanted to look at it.

Because Worth said the sword was magic, and the blacksmith who had let him use his forge to create it said Worth had done things he'd never seen before.

"Don't you dare." William didn't turn around, but there was real anger in his voice.

"Hey, chubby," Riley shot back, "you control your sword and I'll control mine."

Riley grabbed the hilt and pulled it from its sheath. She wasn't comfortable with this, but she wanted to know what Lucie thought. Lucie had magic and could actually *use* it.

Maybe she could see more about the sword than Riley could, because despite what Worth and the blacksmith said, she'd seen no magic.

The only thing different about it was the green lines running through the hilt.

Lucie took the sword from Riley's hands, laying the blade across one palm and the hilt across the other. She did it respectfully, showing reverence and perhaps even awe. She obviously knew what this meant, for a Right Hand to let her touch her sword.

"It looks normal aside from the hilt," Riley observed.

"Aye, it does," Lucie responded. "What did the tent man say? What did he tell you this thing could do?"

Riley stared at the sword. "He didn't really say much, Lucie. Just that it was magic."

"Have you practiced with it?"

Riley nodded. "Three hours each day since he made it. It's important to practice with every sword, even one you know like your hand, but a new one? You have to use it for countless hours if you're going to have a chance of surviving."

"Aye, why?"

"It has to become an extension of you," Riley answered. "It has to become your *hand*."

"What happened when you used this one?"

Riley knew right then something was different about the sword, even if she'd denied it before. Because this sword…

"I didn't need to practice with it."

"Whatcha mean?" William turned around. "Ain't need to practice?"

"*Now* you want in on the convo after you told me not to hand it over?" Riley smirked.

"Just tell me whatcha mean, skinny. Every swordsman has to practice."

Riley looked at the sword, feeling real awe. "It's hard to explain. It just…fit me like a glove. It seems to almost anticipate where I'm going to go, which means *it* moves quicker and with more force. I know that doesn't make any sense, but learning the weight of it, the feel of it, the *control* of it…I already know all that."

"But you kept practicin'. I seen ya. That don't make no sense," William told her.

"I practiced because I don't really believe it. I practiced because that's what a Right Hand does, but the sword just feels different."

"Aye." Lucie handed it back to Riley. "The sword is definitely different."

"How?" Riley asked as she sheathed it.

"I can't really say. You'll have to find out on your own.

I'd venture to guess that whatever is there is between you and it, me and even the tent man can't say what that is."

"Bullshit. That's a sword with some green lines, and you both sound like mad hens."

Lucie looked at Riley. "Does he *ever* shut up?"

"I'm afraid not. It's like this pretty much all the time."

William turned around. "Being alone with you two on a ship sounds almost as fun as drowning myself."

CHAPTER TWO

"I can't hurt you, Mason. You understand that, right?"

Mason didn't look at Rendal but rather stared at the rows of people standing on the ship's deck.

"It's not that I don't *want* to. You shouldn't ever believe that. You and your bloodline owe me a debt, and I'm going to collect it."

The mage stepped away from Mason, walking a bit farther down the deck. "But, if I hurt you, she's not going to join me. If she shows up and you're injured, or worse, dead, I can kiss that goodbye. I am prepared for that if it comes to it...but I don't *want* it, you know?"

Rendal turned around and looked at Mason.

"She's much more valuable to me if she's on my side willingly, not like the people behind me."

Mason didn't understand who the hell stood behind Rendal. Mason had been on the ship for a week, but this was the first time he'd been above decks. They'd kept him in a room next to the mage's, and he had hardly seen anyone.

Now, though, he stood beneath the sun and heard the waves slapping against the ship's sides.

Fifty people stood in front of him, although none looked to be...

In control, he thought. *They all look like they're in some kind of trance.*

The people stared straight forward, blinking occasionally. Each wore a dark red necklace, though none were lit. Rendal had the same color bracelet on his right wrist.

"So, Mason," the mage continued, "unfortunately, I have to make sure you're in good shape as we go forward. At least until she decides to join, then I can do what I'd like to."

Mason's eyes flashed to the mage. "She'll never join you. Don't you see that? You can kidnap Lucie and me. You can take William, and even my father. You can burn down New Perth, but Riley isn't going to join *you*."

Mason almost laughed at the ridiculousness of this man. He understood Rendal's power, but not his insanity. To think—after everything—that Riley would join him?

"Come, let's look off the side of the ship," the mage instructed.

Mason wanted to ask about the people standing around, but it would only show weakness. The mage had brought him up here to show him these people...but he wasn't ready to explain it yet.

Mason followed Rendal to the rail of the ship. He saw only the ocean in all directions and had no idea where he was.

"We came from that way." Rendal pointed to his right. "And New Perth is that way." His hand moved across the horizon. "At on this very day, your Right Hand is stepping onto a ship that will come to us."

Mason swallowed. He knew Rendal could see things, which shouldn't be possible. Out here in the ocean, the mage knew what was happening in New Perth.

"They've got a crew of both soldiers and magicians, I think," Rendal continued. "Lucie is being a real bitch and trying to block my ability to see, her and that other mage. It's making things blurry, but they're simply no match for me."

"They're coming?"

"Of course!" Rendal was happy. "That's the whole *point!*"

"You've got to know she won't join you." Mason shook his head, suddenly depressed. He hadn't known exactly what Rendal's plan was, only that he—Mason—would most likely die. He hadn't truly thought Riley would come for him out here, or anyone else in New Perth—not over this ocean that stretched forever.

"You keep saying that, Mason, and I'm beginning to wonder if you're actually paying attention. She *already* came with me once. That was the whole plan. That's what the plan has been the entire time."

Mason knew it was true. Riley had agreed to go with the mage in exchange for his word that he wouldn't attack New Perth.

"Yes, you're seeing it correctly." Rendal nodded, smiling. The mage was clearly reading Mason's mind. "She came when she thought it would save New Perth. That was step one. And I was with her for a few days, Mason, as you well know. I came to understand her better during that time. Her connection to New Perth is strong, but not *nearly* as strong as her connection to you. She was willing to die for New Perth, but for Mason Ire, heir to the Prefect's throne? Oh, goodness. The things she'll do..."

Mason gripped the rail, his knuckles turning white.

"Because you see, Mason, I need her to *change*, and with you as my captive, I can make that happen."

Mason shook his head. "No. She won't. Not for me. Not for anything."

"You don't know her like I do, because despite how much you care, you can't walk through her mind. I can. I have. I've gone inside the rooms she keeps bolted, and I know what she'll sacrifice for you. Her very soul."

"You're going to die."

It was all Mason could think to say.

"We're going to kill you."

The mage laughed. "Oh, good times, Mason. Good times indeed. Now look, I didn't just come up here to torture you with what's to come for Ms. Riley, although that was part of the fun. Here, take this."

Rendal pulled a small telescope from his robe's pocket and handed it to Mason. "Look out there."

Mason extended the telescope to its full length and pointed it in the direction Rendal indicated.

"See them?"

Mason did. A ship, but not Riley's. There was a flag flying over it, a banner Mason didn't understand.

"Them there's pirates." Rendal spoke in a fake country accent. "They comin' to steal our gold and take our wimmen. Gonna to take our ship, too." He laughed.

He dropped the accent. "I brought you up here so you can see what happens. They're still a day or so away, but they're heading right for us. Their ship is faster than ours, so even if I wanted to run, I couldn't get away." He looked at Mason. "You don't know much about the seas, do you? Much like magic, you Prefects have never had much use for anything that's not on land."

Mason shook his head, still staring at the ship. They were coming for them, that was for sure. The flag was black, and the ship looked ruthless, like some long dead skeleton that wanted vengeance.

"The seas are a dangerous place if you don't know what you're doing. Harold, my head guard—he's had a lot of experience on the ocean. And me… Well, you've seen what I'm capable of. But those pirates claim this part of the sea, and that means they are going to try and kill us, then rape any women aboard. Claiming rights is their way of trying to sound just."

Mason put the telescope down, not wanting to look at the ship anymore. "What the hell does that have to do with me? If they're coming to kill us and we're going to die, why show it to me now?"

"We're not going to die, Assistant Prefect. Goodness, no! Those men *are* cutthroats, though. They make their living… Hell, they *exist* by having no conscience. Indeed, few land dwellers would survive against the ocean's deadliest creatures—and not all of them are below water. No, Mason, you're here now so that in a day's time, you can see what happens to those very, very dangerous men."

Mason closed the telescope, not looking at the mage.

"Because before this is over, you're going to tell Riley to join me. You're going to see that it's absolutely hopeless to do anything else. She can't stand against me, and if she tries, you'll die, and she'll end up on my side anyway. So pay attention, Assistant Prefect. You'll want to know the truth of all this when she gets here."

Rendal put the Assistant Prefect back in his room, then retired to his own chambers.

"Harold, what's the best guess as to when those pirates will be on us?"

Harold stood in the doorway. "Tomorrow afternoon, sir."

"Good. I want to be very clear here, Harold, so that there are no mix-ups. I don't want anyone to interfere when they arrive. Your orders are to let them board our ship, and even if they kill some of our men, you're not to attack. Understand?"

"Yes, sir. I understand completely."

Rendal nodded. He moved to the bar cabinet and pulled out a bottle of dark liquor. His quarters were well stocked, even if the rest of his crew's weren't. He poured himself a drink and took a sip, feeling the liquid burn all the way down.

"They're on the way, Harold. Do you think they see it? How I'm making them repeat this pattern? That they keep having to come for me again and again?"

Harold shook his head. "I doubt it, sir. The more I realize how lost I was in this whole thing, the more I believe everyone must be lost as well. None can even try to catch up, because they're simply too far behind."

Rendal took another sip. "Now you see the truth,

Harold. I knew you'd come around." He smiled. Harold was a good man, even if he'd gotten a bit confused about the whole Riley situation. "This time we'll battle on the sea, but I won't take her with us. She'll crack a little more, but she's not going to break. Not yet. She's strong, and even with Mason pitching in it'll take more. But that's fine, Harold. I've got time."

He turned around and looked at his second-in-command.

"What New Perth didn't understand when they kicked me out was that this isn't a sprint. It's a marathon. Riley doesn't know that yet either. She thinks this next battle will end the war, but it's only a stepping-stone to something higher, Harold. Pay attention this time, my friend. I don't want to lose you again."

The mage's voice held no warmth even as he smiled at his head guard. He wanted him to understand only one message: you get no more chances.

Rendal stepped out on the expansive deck. He looked no more like a captain than a kangaroo did. He wore his robe, despite the sun blazing above.

Before him, a smaller ship floated in front of his larger one. It was parallel, and ladders had been extended from their deck to his.

"Ah, here we are," he told Mason who stood on his right side.

"Do you ever get bored with your theatrics?"

"No, sir," Rendal answered. "It's the theatrics that give

me the most fun. The more important question is, are you ready to see what I can do when your friends show up? Are you ready to see what's going to happen to New Perth?"

"You do whatever you need to right now, Rendal, to make yourself feel powerful. Riley *is* coming, though, and when she gets here, you're going to have a very different outlook on things, I think."

"We'll see, we'll see." Rendal stepped up to Harold, leaving the Assistant Prefect behind him. "How are our new friends doing?"

"You heard them from belowdecks?"

Rendal nodded. "Yes." It'd been something less than pleasantries—a warning cannonball flying over the ship and disappearing into the ocean.

"Well, not much else so far. Took them a bit to line up with us, and now we're just waiting for them to board."

The deck was empty, all of the men below. Rendal knew they weren't happy; many were actually terrified. He didn't care.

A man stepped out of a hatch onto the deck of the pirate ship. He was dirty, with long stringy, black hair. He wore a bandanna and had a large scar across the left side of his face. He held a thin sword in his right hand and looked to have about nine different knives hanging from a belt around his waist.

"Aye, my name is Captain Grayskull, and this here is my ship. These here are my men."

And as he spoke the last few words, some of the grimiest human beings Rendal had ever seen came up from belowdecks. They spread out around their captain, all wearing black and brown tattered clothing. Some were toothless, some had only one eye, some only one leg.

"They make mutants look healthy, don't they, Harold?" Rendal laughed.

"Yes, sir. I'd say your assessment is correct."

The pirates all held weapons, and more kept emerging.

"Now, I have the rights to this here water you're floating on, and I didn't receive me necessary paperwork to sign off on. That means you are sailing illegally in my waters."

The pirates on the other deck laughed.

"So, without the paperwork," the captain continued, "I'm afraid I'mma have to take possession of this ship and all the loot on it."

"Aye!" someone shouted. "Need to take possession!"

The crew laughed again.

The captain still hadn't moved from his ship. The ladders connecting the ships remained empty.

Rendal decided to play dumb. "Where would I get the paperwork you speak of, Captain Grayskull?"

"Aye, the paperwork. Men, where would he get the paperwork? I can't remember where I put it."

"I think it might be up me ass!" someone shouted.

"No, no, you put it up Brett's ass last night!"

The captain laughed along with his crew, but as his smile faded, their laughter died.

"I guess it's up someone's ass over here, from the sound of things. Either way, I didn't get it in time, so I'm going to be comin' aboard that ship, and then you all are gonna do what I say. You understand me?"

Rendal looked at Harold. "He's making some serious demands, isn't he?"

"Yes, sir. It would appear we should listen to them."

"Aye, if you two are over there makin' jokes, I suggest you stop. Now, before we board, how many men ya got?"

"How many would you say, Harold?"

"Besides us three?" Harold asked with a grin.

"Yes, besides us three." Rendal didn't take his eyes from the pirate captain as he joked with his second-in-command.

"Well, if we include the ones we got in chains, plus your private army, I'd have to put the number at five hundred or so."

"Enough!" the captain screamed across the expanse. "Men, take them!"

"Mason, friend, pay attention." Rendal's voice carried to the Assistant Prefect's ears.

The pirates rushed forward and climbed the ladders. Loud grunts and angry curses filled the air, but Rendal and Harold remained in place.

The bracelet on Rendal's wrist lit, shining deep red for everyone to see. He closed his eyes, and the nanocytes in his blood latched onto those of the people wearing the necklaces. He could feel their bodies as if they were his own, the energy inside them now his to control.

Artino had explained how it worked to him. The amphoralds in his bracelet were charged with his energy, and he was using them to control others. Through the amphoralds, his nanocytes were focusing those inside his prisoners, their potential becoming his.

It was like mind control, but he only needed to tell the

bracelet on his wrist what to do instead of fifty people at once. Rendal directed his will to the bracelet, and it sang that across the necklaces on his prisoners.

They were his to do with as he wished.

The first of the pirates reached his ship, but Rendal still didn't move. The captain climbed his ladder carefully, slowly, even as those around him rushed up the others.

"Belowdecks, lads. That's where we'll find 'em."

"Indeed, it is," Rendal whispered.

Two large hatches opened on the ship's deck, basically holes with ladders leading down.

The pirates running across the deck skidded across the wood as they came to a stop.

"What the hell?"

Red eyes peered up from below. Fifty pairs of them.

"Captain!" one of the pirates shouted. "Captain, ya need to see this!"

Captain Grayskull landed on Rendal's ship with a *thud*.

"What's stoppin' you?" he screamed. "Move outta the way!"

He shoved forward, pushing people out of the way. The two hatches in the deck were just in front of Rendal and Harold, separating them from the cutthroats holding knives, swords, and axes. None of their eyes were on Rendal, though.

They stared at these new people.

"What's wrong with their eyes?"

Rendal smiled. "You see, Harold? Things are never as bad as they seem, are they?"

"No, sir. Not with you."

"What the hell?" the captain asked. Having made his

way to the doors, he was now looking down at the unmoving people.

Their faces were lax, their eyes calm, their pupils glowing red.

"Gentleman, this is part of my crew. Would you like to meet them?"

The captain glanced at Rendal. "What's wrong with their eyes?"

"What on Earth do you mean?"

"You know damn well what I mean. Why are they red? And why are they wearing those necklaces? They're glowin' red too!"

"Would you like to see?"

"Don't you move! Don't you *dare* move! Men, seize 'im!" the captain demanded.

The pirates didn't move an inch. They all stood staring at their leader and this strange robed man, unsure what to do.

Rendal walked behind Harold and then headed to the rail, skirting both hatches and the group of pirates around them.

"That's a good looking ship, Captain Grayskull. Fast too, huh? No way mine could have gotten away from it."

"You listen to me right now, and you listen good. Don't move another step 'less you want me to pop your head off your neck like a zit on my ass, you understand?"

Rendal raised his hand next to his face and looked at the palm.

"I wonder…how's a pirate to survive without a ship?" Rendal asked. The whole pirate crew stared at him now, their eyes distrusting and their hands tight on their weapons.

Rendal closed his hand slightly, his fingers shaking as if he suddenly held some immeasurably hard rock.

A loud groaning sound filled the open air. Wood creaking.

"NO!" the captain shouted, rushing back to the rail, knowing exactly where the noise came from.

"Harold," Rendal called. "Start us moving at full speed. We don't want to get sucked down with it."

"Yes, sir."

"And Harold, let's make the pirates feel at home. How would *they* say such a thing?"

Harold smiled. "Aye aye, Captain."

Harold disappeared down the ladder, the red-eyed army moving out of the way for him before shifting back into their spaces.

Rendal's hand closed tighter, and things started popping on the other ship. Loud noises that sounded like explosions. Wood cracking and breaking.

"*KILL HIM!*" the captain shouted, pointing his sword at Rendal. The pirates' trance broke. Whatever this mage was doing, he had to be stopped.

They rushed forward, and Rendal's red bracelet shone over the entire deck.

It sounded like a cannon fired from the two hatches.

The men rushing toward Rendal were blindsided, but not by fire. Not by electricity. Not by anything that could hurt Rendal's ship.

Instead, wind slammed into them and they flew through the air, knocking into each other, some skidding across the wooden deck. They hit the rail, cracking their ribs and arms and shoulders.

Shouts rang out.

More rushed forward, the wind not stopping them all. The ship had begun moving, the ladders pulling away from the pirate ship.

Rendal's fist closed more, and the first true sounds of breaking came. Water was flooding in through the hull, and splintered wood burst from the ship's sides, flying into the ocean. Water churned as the ladders fell between the two ships.

Some of the pirates rushed to the rail to view the ship that was being left behind.

Rendal's soldiers were all on deck now, their eyes bright red.

A pirate was five feet from Rendal, his sword out and his face full of fury.

Rendal didn't move, only closed his hand a bit tighter, the invisible rock crumbling.

The pirate stopped in his tracks as if he had run into a brick wall. His sword moved against his will, the point now facing his gut.

One of Rendal's red-eyed soldiers stood behind him, face emotionless, hands at his sides.

The pirate plunged the sword into his own stomach, his blood spilling on the deck.

Rendal smiled and glanced across the ship at Mason.

"You see, Assistant Prefect?"

Rendal's hand closed more, and the staff holding the pirates' flag shattered and dropped shards of wood onto the broken deck.

The soldiers were tossing pirates over the rail, using a combination of wind and telekinesis.

Screams and blood.

Rendal only smiled, his hand closing farther and more easily as the ship's internal structure fell apart, the sea claiming it.

And then his hand was fully closed and the pirate ship was sinking.

Half his soldiers turned their attention to the ship's sails.

A huge wind suddenly filled them. The ship had been moving before, but now it truly took off. The pirate ship continued going down behind them, but the water couldn't suck Rendal's ship down with it. They were too far away.

Rendal watched as Captain Grayskull was tossed over the rail. He screamed as he fell.

The mage turned from the rail and strode across the deck to where Mason stood. Painful yells still filled the air, but they were growing fewer and fewer.

Mason's eyes didn't hold the fear that Rendal had hoped for, but he cared little. Time was on his side.

"Are you seeing what I mean yet?"

He stood so that the two men were shoulder to shoulder, watching the melee play out in front of them. Another pirate was flung into the ocean, the screams ending as he hit the water.

"I see you're a cruel man, mage or not. I know that if Riley is coming for me, she's not bringing cruelty but justice. It's going to be cold when it gets here, Rendal. At least as cold as the water you just tossed those men into."

CHAPTER THREE

Riley didn't like being on a ship one bit. William had warned her, but she hadn't listened—mainly because she didn't have a choice. If Rendal was on the ocean, then Riley had to be on the ocean too.

She hadn't known how *much* she would hate it, though.

Her stomach was in constant turmoil and her head felt like it was always swimming, her brain trying to stay above some waterline it hadn't known about.

"Weaker both on land and on water." William laughed and slapped his knee as Riley bent over the bucket at the side of her chair.

"I'll show you weak—"

She tried to say something back to him, but the food she'd eaten an hour ago shot up her throat. She stared at the mess for a moment, wiping her mouth with the back of her arm before straightening.

Riley, William, Lucie, and Worth were three levels below the upper deck.

"Laugh all you want, William, but I know you didn't eat lunch just so you'd avoid this." Lucie's smirk filled her face.

"I did no such thing."

"Oh, yeah? Tell me, then, why there is twice as much food left in the kitchen as there normally would be?"

"Enough." William grunted. "We've got stuff to teach the young lady."

Lucie laughed, knowing that she'd won. William didn't want people to see him vomiting, and it would certainly curtail his ability to make fun of Riley.

"I forgot that you're a master mage already," Lucie retorted. "Go on then, William. Show her what to do. Please."

The crew had set sail one day ago, and the lessons had already started.

Worth had told it short and simple. "No time. Make you magic now or we die."

Lucie was a mage, too, but she'd taken a back seat to Worth's teaching so far.

"You stubborn." Worth refused to stop for Riley's stomach. "More stubborn than him."

He pointed at William.

The big man grinned at Riley. "So stubborn, Riley. Be more like me. Pliable. Easily molded."

Riley gritted her teeth. "Don't forget what happened when Rendal kept fucking with me, William. You want to see me explode?"

"I'm much too powerful for that now, Riley. Child's play." William's grin was large enough to split his face.

"Focus," Worth snapped. "Here. Now. He know we come. He see us right now, so you focus."

Riley did; she forced away her rolling stomach and hurting head. She wanted to learn this. She *needed* to learn this. For her own sake, but also for New Perth's. For Mason's.

"Sword important for him. Not you. Magic greater in you. Because it greater, your focus must be greater. Eyes closed."

Riley listened.

She'd been doing this for hours, and so far nothing had happened. No fire in her hands like William. No red eyes. Nothing.

Even now with her eyes closed, she couldn't focus like she did with her sword. There was no physical extension of her. Nothing for her senses to latch onto. Nowhere for her mind to *go*. It was forced to be silent and focus only on itself.

"What you see?"

"Nothing. Just blackness."

"Deeper."

"What do you mean, Worth?"

"Deeper. Go deeper."

Riley simply sat with her eyes shut, not understanding.

"What you see?"

"The same. Just blackness."

The big bald man was growing frustrated and he stood up, nearly knocking over his stool. "Enough for now. Need rest. Me. You need think. Figure out what you want."

Worth left the room, saying nothing else.

William stood. "I ain't never seen him that upset. You must really be pissing him off, skinny."

"I...I don't know how. I'm trying my hardest. I really am. I just don't know what he wants."

"I'm gonna go grab some—" William stopped mid-sentence, looking at them.

"Grab some what?" Lucie smirked.

They both knew how he'd been about to end the sentence. Grab some *food*.

"Just some stuff." He walked out of the room, not looking at either of them.

"That man has more pride than anyone but Rendal himself." Lucie stood and lifted her stool up, then brought it over to Riley. "He's teaching you to do it differently than I learned."

"Worth?"

"Well, certainly not William. He couldn't teach a thief to steal, far as I can tell."

"How did you learn? Who taught you?"

"Rendal did. I think that's why I fell in love with him. I was only twenty." Lucie looked down at her shoes. "I think the love was based quite a bit on what he saw in me. Something I didn't understand myself at the time. He used me. I see that now. Like he wants to use you."

She looked back up.

"You know that, right?"

Riley nodded. "He told me. He said he wants me to be his heir."

"That's what he told you, but don't you believe him, girl. Rendal don't want no heir. Rendal don't think he's ever gonna die."

"What's he really want, then?" Riley asked.

"Same thing all men with power want—to get more

power. He'll use you to help him do it. This is tough for ya now, learning how to let the magic loose inside you, but Rendal is right. The amount you hold...I saw it the first day I met you. Unleashing it might be hard, but when you do, it's going to rip through this whole continent, girl. It's going to *change* things."

"I don't care about any of that. I don't care about changing the continent, or even New Perth. I just want to get Mason back. That's why I'm doing this."

"I know." She stood up and walked across the room. "I can tell you how Rendal taught me if you think it might help."

"I'll take any advice you have right now. Absolutely any."

Lucie nodded, grinning. "I don't care what Worth says. Ya ain't as stubborn as that big dumb animal William." She went to the other side of the room and spread her arms to either side, the smile fading from her face. "Rendal used to tell me that it's all energy. Magic isn't anything other than that. Energy is matter, and some people—special people, as he used to call us—can bend it to their will. It's not really magic at all. There's something different about us that lets us manipulate the physical world, and that includes minds, because make no mistake, it's energy inside your brain right now, girl."

"It's not magic?"

"It's magic to the people that don't understand it. Worth calls it magic, but I don't think he really believes that. To him and his kind, it's the same as breathing. They just know how to do it. Think about it like this: if someone hadn't seen you with your sword before, and you came on an army at night, sweepin' down on 'em like the damned wind, what do you think they would call you the next day?"

"A ghost," Riley answered.

"Exactly. Simply because people wouldn't understand how it's possible. Because a human shouldn't be able to do that. In reality, you're made out of flesh and blood just like them, only you've practiced and honed your skills. That's what this is: it's a skill, one that can be practiced. Instead of flippin' your sword around, you're flippin' energy."

Riley shook her head, staring at the floor in front of her. "Worth just tells me to focus; that I'll find it if I do. That's what William said he did. Said he just focused and started seeing my face, and poof, his hands were on fire."

"Focus is in an important part, but it wasn't what Rendal told me was the most important."

"And what was that?" Riley asked.

"A goal. The first time he had me create magic, he wanted me to move a rock. Nothing big, just a pebble. He wanted me to pick it up and move it from one edge of the table to the other. He said I had to see the end first. That to see the rock where it currently was would only make it harder."

Riley's eyes narrowed. "My only goal is to get Mason back."

Lucie grinned. "All this concern for Mason! I wonder if maybe ye ain't wantin' a bit more than to only be his Right Hand."

"No!" Riley shouted, mortified.

"I'm kiddin' ya, girl. Calm down before you bring the whole ship in here. Now look." Lucie moved her head, nodding at the lamps on the walls that lit the room. "I want those candles to darken, so I first see it in my mind. I see the room growing darker. I see the shadows creeping across your face. I see…"

But then they were in it. The room was *darker*. Riley looked at the lamps, which had grown very dim. One was out.

"You try," Lucie said. "Try to bring them back to life."

Riley nodded and closed her eyes. She focused all her attention on the lights she saw in her mind. They were dark, and she wanted them to be brighter. She watched as the flames grew taller inside her head, the lamps driving away all the shadows in the room.

Yes, it was working.

She saw the room as she wanted it.

Riley opened her eyes.

Shadows still reigned around her. Lucie still stood across the room, her face troubled.

"It's okay," she whispered. "I promise. The potential is in you, and there's nothing that you can do about that. There's no way to put a cap on the bottle."

"I need to be able to use it, though. To *direct* it. My sword, even with whatever Worth has done to it, won't be enough."

"Hush now. I don't wanna hear nothin' else like that." Lucie walked across the room. She put her hand on Riley's shoulder. "I pulled you from the street when you were nothin' but an urchin without two coins to rub together. Now you're a Right Hand, one of only two. You've been enough your whole damned life, and you're gonna *keep* being enough. I know Rendal. I know him better'n anyone else walkin' this Earth, and the reason he wants you so bad is that you're better'n him. You're better'n he'll ever be."

Riley tilted her head up and looked at Lucie.

"You're gonna be a mage different from those before ya. You're gonna change things, and it don't matter at all that you ain't brightening the lights right now."

"I don't care, as long as I save Mason."

The door behind them opened, and they glanced at it.

"I hope you two are done talkin' 'bout your knittin' or whatever you women do." William grinned, clearly thinking himself clever. "But we got trouble above."

Lucie looked at Riley again. "Even if you don't ever get nowhere with magic, I promise I'll teach you some things that'll make his balls fall right off."

Riley climbed the ladder to the upper deck. The moon shone brightly across the tossing waves. Riley was glad the weather was good because she didn't think she could handle much more movement.

"What is it?" she asked.

Verith stood at the deck's edge, leaning against the rail. He held a long telescope to his eye.

"He's the man to talk to," William told her.

Riley walked toward the man, William following. Worth was already next to Verith. The wind rushed over them all, chilly now that the sun had set.

"Pirates," Verith commented as Riley approached.

"You can see them from here?"

"Just barely, but the lookout in the crow's nest saw them and sent someone to get me."

"Do you have experience sailing, Verith?" Riley asked.

"Aye, I do. Part of the training for New Perth's military. Can't be the highest general of the kingdom without knowing how to operate ships."

"See, Riley, it's not all about brawn. You got to have brains too if you want to make it in this world." William laughed.

"Shut it or you're goin' over, chubby." Riley turned her attention back to Verith. "How far off are the pirates?"

"Tough to say in the dark like this."

"I make light. You want?" Worth asked from the other side of Verith. He still seemed grumpy, although he did hold a chalice in his left hand.

"That's not a bad idea if you can do it, Worth, although I need to think through the ramifications."

"You know what that word means, skinny?" William asked, grinning.

"The adults are speaking," Riley zipped back at him. "If you light the sky up, Worth, they're going to know we have magic onboard."

"Exactly," Verith agreed. "Which means when they get here, they might just shoot cannonballs at us and sink us rather than risk dealing with mages."

"So, no light?" Worth asked.

"No, I don't think so. Tomorrow we'll know better how close they are. They won't reach us tonight."

"Good." Worth brought the chalice to his lips and took a deep drink of the wine. "Riley give me headache. Need rest."

He gave the Right Hand a goofy-looking wink and walked off, leaving the three to themselves.

"Trouble with the training?" Verith asked.

"She just ain't as good as me." William smirked.

"Verith, if we feed him to sharks, do you think the Prefect will understand?" Riley asked.

Verith smiled. "I wouldn't presume to speak for Prefect Ire." His smile faded. "We're going to have to figure out what to do about those pirates."

"What do they want?" Riley asked.

"Pirates only want a couple of things: loot and women."

"Will our New Perth flag dissuade them from pursuing such desires?"

Verith still held the telescope to his eye as he shook his head. "No. On the sea, New Perth holds no sway. The pirates know they can sink this ship and simply sail off into the horizon without having to worry about vengeance from New Perth."

Riley stared out into the dark ocean, unable to see what Verith was looking at.

"We'll have time tomorrow." Verith closed the telescope and slipped it into the pocket on his shirt. "We just need to make sure we're all up first thing in the morning."

"That means no sleepin' in, Riley. Get your ass up early." William was truly having a great time with the fact that he could practice magic and she couldn't.

"You shouldn't want me waking up too early, jackass, because *you* might not wake up at all," Riley quipped.

"Yeah, yeah. Come on. We all need some sleep. We'll deal with the pirates tomorrow morning."

The sun was bright above, and William didn't feel as sick as he had the night before. Of course, he wouldn't tell Riley or Lucie such a thing; he'd never hear the end of it. William knew he gave them way too much shit—even if he was always joking—to show any weakness.

Worth was standing on the poop deck, and William made his way over. He could see the pirate ship in the distance, and it was definitely gaining on them. He hadn't had time to talk to Verith yet this morning, but he trusted the general. The man was doing everything in his power to make sure the crew would be safe.

Worth had been standing up there for quite some time, just staring. A few of the tent mages had come and spoken to him, but the conversations had been brief.

"Hey, Worth." William leaned against the rail in front of both men.

"Hi."

"Wanted to talk to you about a few things, if you got the time."

William had seen this man as beneath him when they had first met. Worth had been leading a group of mutants out of the desert. He realized he'd been foolish, though. This man was wise and knew more than William probably ever would.

Again, he wouldn't admit such a thing to Riley or Lucie. They'd hound him until the end of time.

"Got time. Nothing *but* time 'til we meet mage again."

"Well, first, why the hell are you staring at that ship so

hard? I don't really see them being that big of a hindrance to us. I don't think Verith does either."

"Aye, mayhap not." Worth didn't smile, which bothered William. The man always smiled.

"Then why ya staring?"

"Something different."

"About it?"

"Aye." Worth nodded. "Somethin' different, betcha."

"Something to be worried about?"

"Can't see. Tryin' to, but can't."

"You talked to Verith this morning? Did he say when they'll be here?"

Worth nodded again. "Aye, be here tomorrow morn."

William wasn't going to worry about the pirates. A bunch of ragtag cutthroats could be easily dispatched, and to be honest, he wanted the struggle. It'd been too long since he'd had a real fight and he felt a bit rusty.

"Now, Worth, what I want to talk to you about next, you can't tell no one, you understand?"

Worth looked at him. William grinned; the man's lips were still purple from the wine he had drunk the previous night.

"I mean, it ain't bad, Worth. Don't look like that. But you know how Riley will get if she knows somethin' about me. She'll tease until she dies from laughter."

"Aye. Know how you are, too. You do same."

William laughed. "I suppose I do. But seriously, keep this between us, okay?"

"Aye. Worth not tell."

"First, I want more magic training. The fire is good, but I want to do more. Is that possible?"

"Aye. Possible. You stubborn, but it possible."

William nodded. He was glad to hear it. "I know that training Riley is most important, but can we make time over the next few days?"

"Aye, Worth make time for ya."

"Thanks." William stared at the coming ship and his smile faded. "The next thing is about Riley. I know you use magic. I know your tent people use magic. But I've seen Rendal twice, and I know how strong he is. You and I both have lost people close to us facing him, and from what I understand, we need Riley to stop him. That about right?"

"Aye, mayhap. He strong."

William thought he could see the pirate's flag, although he couldn't make out exactly what was on it.

"So, is she going to learn how to do this? Do you think you'll be able to get through to her?"

Worth turned to him, his eyebrows scrunching together. He looked at William for long seconds and then smiled wildly, looking like the Worth William knew.

"She magic, big man. She more magic than you. Than me. There no 'get through.' There no worry."

"You were worried before we got on this ship?" William straightened, growing to his full height as he turned to the bald man.

"I worried?"

"Hell, yeah, you worried! You didn't want to go and sulked like a child." William felt his temper rising. Worth was acting like he wasn't concerned and never had been.

"Oh..." He nodded, still grinning. "Act, big man. All act. Need to make her think."

He tapped the side of his head with his finger.

"Pressure. Create diamond. You see?"

William felt his anger draining, a grin slowly replacing it. "Mind games?"

Worth raised his hand and tilted it back and forth.

"But she'll be okay?"

"Yes, big man. She okay. She magic. She just fine."

Worth turned from him and looked back at the sea.

"You're worried about that ship?"

Worth didn't move. He only said, "Something different."

CHAPTER FOUR

The ship arrived the next morning, just as Worth said it would.

Riley was on the deck, standing behind Verith, who, while not officially, was the ship's captain. Worth stood to her left and William to her right. Lucie waited to the right of William.

Behind them stood about fifty soldiers, plus a handful of mages Worth had brought up.

"Think we'll need them?" Riley had asked.

"Can't say." That had been all Worth *would* say.

Riley easily saw what was on the other deck, and it sent a chill down her spine.

The same green stones that lined her sword were *everywhere.* Inside the hull. On the deck. On the lookout. She still saw no one, only looked on in amazement as the ship glistened green beneath the bright sun above.

"Worth, you need to tell them what all that is."

She saw him nod out of the corner of her eye.

"They..." He paused, bringing his hand to his face and

rubbing his bare chin. She knew the sign well; it meant he was trying to figure out how to explain what was in his head. "They energy."

"Magic?"

"No. Not magic. Energy."

"Riley, I need you to get this desert dweller to start making sense." William grunted.

Riley sent a sharp elbow into William's side. He sucked in air and grinned as he looked down at her.

"They...tech...What word?"

"Technology?" Verith said from up front.

Worth nodded. "Yes. They technology, those green stones. Energy. Not magic, but close."

"Is it dangerous?" Verith asked.

Another nod.

Fire lit William's hands. His sword remained across his back, but she thought he was getting more comfortable with simply using the fire to fight.

She wouldn't say anything, knowing it would embarrass him, but she was proud all the same.

He could still do more than she, but Riley was getting better at it by the day.

"They're as dangerous as Riley," William quipped, still grinning though now staring at the pirate ship. "Which is to say, not very. I'll run through 'em like shit through a kangaroo."

She gave him another sharp elbow.

"Hey!" He started, patting his left arm with his right hand and putting out the flames on his shirt. "Careful!"

She laughed, unable to help herself.

"Okay, focus, everyone," Verith commanded.

And as their ship quieted, a woman stepped onto the deck on the other.

"Holy hell," William whispered.

"Keep your pants buttoned up." Riley knew exactly what William was thinking. The woman was stunning. She didn't look like any pirate Riley had ever imagined.

Her hair was thick and full, and blazing red. She wore older black leather, but it was tight and fit her body perfectly. Lacework crossed the front, although her ample bosom was easily seen.

"We don't need to fight her," William whispered. "We need to—"

"Father and Mother, he's done gone and fell in love," Lucie interrupted.

William was quiet, clearly stunned by the woman's beauty. To be fair, Riley was too. She'd never seen anyone like her.

"This what you meant, Worth?" William finally managed to say. "Something different? Is *she* what's different?"

"Or maybe it's the ship with the green stones running through it, ya big animal?" Lucie offered good-naturedly.

"Something different." Worth said nothing else.

The woman moved an instrument to her mouth that Riley had never seen before, a cone of sorts with a handle on it. The handle held green stones. The woman pressed a button and then spoke into the cone's small end.

Her voice soared across the expanse, although the woman showed no effort at all.

"I'm Captain Erin Stormhandle, and this is my ship.

That ship you're on, the one beneath your feet right now—that one is mine, too. You just don't know it yet."

Riley put her hand on her sword.

She stepped forward, moving past Verith to the rail.

"I'm Right Hand Riley Trident, and what I *do* know is that if you don't turn that ship around and go back to whatever hellhole you came from, the only other place you'll be going is the bottom of this ocean."

The redhaired woman smiled brilliantly.

A man walked up on her right.

"No fuckin' way." William stepped up to Riley's side. "You got a fuckin' twin, skinny?"

Riley's mouth opened slightly because the resemblance —at least from this distance—was impossible. The man had short blonde hair, just like hers. He was slim, yet moved with a grace that Riley saw in few others.

"Since you spoke first, you can decide whether to accept my offer." The redhaired woman was still smiling. "You see, I don't prefer all-out battle when it can be avoided. We would win, obviously—all you need do is look at my ship and compare it with yours—but a lot of destruction comes with that. Why don't we do it the old-fashioned way?"

"What way is that?" Riley called to the other ship.

"Your best warrior against my best warrior. Whoever wins gets both ships."

"Hell, yes, I'll take that bet!" William yelled.

"Not yours to take, big man. You weren't the first to speak. Lady there did, so she gets to make the decision. Both if she accepts and then who fights."

The vein in William's neck popped.

He turned around and looked at Riley. "You know I'm the best. I have to fight her."

Riley showed her back to the opposite ship, looking at the rest of the crew. She knew William was angry at being snubbed, but she couldn't let that influence her decision.

Was it her decision? Verith was the de facto ship's captain, yet he looked at her now, as did the others.

"You listenin' to me, skinny? I'm fightin' her."

"First, William, we don't even know if you're fighting her. Let's just think for a moment, okay?"

She heard William's throat click as he swallowed, fighting his instinct to argue.

"Verith, do you know anything about this? What she's talking about? Our best warrior versus hers? I've never heard of it."

Verith nodded. "Yeah, I've heard of it. They practice it a lot on the seas, because truth be told, fighting out here is different. If you lose on land, you can run away. If you lose out here, there isn't anywhere for you to go, so sometimes ship captains will engage in this kind of mini-battle to save a lot of lives."

"What happens to the other ship? To all its people?"

"Usually," Verith continued, "they have the choice of joining the winning ship or going overboard. From what I know, most choose the winning ship."

Riley looked at William. "You won't be fighting her. You know that, right? You'll be fighting the blonde guy who just walked up."

"That's fine. I'll fight both of 'em if I need to."

Riley rolled her eyes. "Don't be silly. *Think*, here. It's not just your pride at stake. It's everyone's life on this ship. It's

Mason's life, and maybe even New Perth's continued existence."

William looked at the people in front of him.

"Sometimes ya gotta listen to her, ya big lug," Lucie encouraged him. "She's smart, and she's right. One on one, your strength ain't nearly as effective as it is in battle."

"Oh, here she is, the cook tellin' me my business."

Riley heard the levity in his voice and knew he was hearing the argument.

"Hell, I bet I could beat that blond better than ya could, William," Lucie shot back.

"Ha!" He turned from her to Riley. "I ain't sayin' you're right, but it seems I'm outnumbered, so it's up to you. You think you can beat that skinny nothing over there?"

Riley didn't look behind her but pictured the man in her mind. They were very similar, but that didn't mean anything.

"Magic," Worth said. "They magic. That powers the green on the ship. Stones."

"You still think you can beat him, skinny? I'm the one who can light my hands on fire."

Riley didn't need to hear any more. She might not be able to use magic, but she also knew if she couldn't beat this guy on the other ship, there wasn't a chance in hell she could beat Rendal.

"I'll take him just fine. You all clear the deck."

She turned toward the red-haired woman. "We accept your challenge. Terms are, we fight on our ship, and that the winner gets all the loot and weapons of the loser. Your men can decide what they want to do after, but we'll have no use for them."

"No use?" William asked from behind.

Riley turned her head around slightly. "We don't need mercenaries fighting for New Perth." She looked at the woman. "That fair?"

"Sure. I'm not too worried about my men, because you're going to die, dear. However, I can tell you're not from the seas, what with that flag you're flying and all. There won't be no fighting on my ship or yours. We fight in the middle, on a ladder."

"See, William," Lucie whispered with glee. "Your fat ass would break the ladder and fall right into the water."

"Shut up, cook," William spat back. "Riley, that's nuts. That's just plain insane, whether or not you're skinny. Tell her to shove that offer up her ass and we'll go to battle like normal, 'cept we got Worth and his mages now."

"That ship," Worth said. "That ship different. They strong. Riley fight. Riley win. More likely."

"Oh, hell." A grin broke across William's face. "We're putting all our faith in Riley's ability to fight on a damned ladder, and hope she doesn't fall in love with that pretty-faced boy over there."

Riley grinned in spite of the situation's seriousness. She jarred William with an elbow.

"*Ooof!*"

"Yeah, keep your mouth shut," she told him before raising her voice. "That sounds fine! Lower the ladder and let's get to this!"

She turned once more to the crew. "Okay, move back. William, don't jump in, no matter what. If you do, the bet is off, and then we'll be at war against a ship I don't understand."

"So if you start losin', you want me to just let you die?" the big man asked.

"I'm not going to lose, William. How many times have I saved *your* ass?"

"Never." He grinned. "Not even once."

"Exactly. Everyone keep their distance. I'll take care of this, and we'll have a new ship in just a few minutes. The only problem is who is going to steer the damned thing."

Riley turned and pulled out her sword as she did. It moved from the sheath easily, making no sound as she revealed it to the world.

The ladder slammed down from the other side, clanging loudly.

Sure enough, she was fighting the blonde. He left his captain, stepping from her and to the ship's rail. The wind whipped them both, jostling their short hair.

The man looked like her, but he wasn't a mirror image, as she'd first thought.

His face was death, which Riley's would never be. His face said he'd killed his whole life because he had to and that one more death on his ledger wasn't going to matter to him in the slightest. He saw Riley as something akin to a piece of furniture that had to be destroyed.

She hardly existed.

Riley smiled inwardly.

Good. Let him underestimate her.

Riley stepped over to the ladder. One side rested on her ship, and the other on theirs. It stretched ten feet onto her ship, giving them leeway if either ship moved, although not a lot.

Her mind was sliding into gear, rapidly assessing her

situation and preparing her body to battle. The ladder was old, and Riley understood that this man would know its weak points a lot better than her. Near his side, she saw a place that looked damaged, yet the middle of the ladder would be the least stable, based on her experience.

The ships were relatively still, but the ladder kept moving. It would move more when they both stepped on.

"Hey, Riley!" William called, "don't trip!"

She laughed. "Fuck you."

Riley stepped onto the ladder, focusing only on her feet. She'd never fought like this before, and none of her training had prepared her for it, either.

The ladder wobbled some. She gently tested a middle bar, seeing if it had been weakened to lure her out.

It held.

When she looked up, the man on the other side was staring back, not even looking at the ladder.

Riley nodded, the steel in her spine coalescing and her mind focusing fully. No jokes. No banter. Just war.

She held her new sword, the green stones sparkling in the sun. It felt good. It felt like it belonged to her.

Her feet started moving, her eyes not needing to look down at them. Her mind was doing it all for her, as it always did. She blazed across the ladder like the wind.

The man on the other side met her, his feet barely touching the wood as he flew toward her.

Their swords clanged when they met. Riley swirled, her feet practically magic, moving around the tiny wooden expanse and circling behind her enemy. He turned easily, meeting her attack with his sword.

His face showed no emotion, no strain—only death.

Riley brought her sword down, finding his already there. She went low, attacking his legs, but he leapt, making her miss. She swept her sword upward, knowing that he would be coming down now.

The *clang* of metal on metal echoed loudly across the ships.

The man came forward, his sword a blur of ferocity. Riley gave ground, perilously close to falling. She parried each attack, but her back was to his ship now and she was moving closer to it.

His attacks were unlike anything she'd ever experienced. Each slice seemed impossibly fast, each cut quicker than the last.

Clang! Clang! Clang!

She met each one, her reflexes perfect as always, her mind still in its killer's state.

Riley suddenly felt heat. She ducked a sweeping cut, glancing behind her quickly.

A wall of fire hung in the air.

Magic.

She could back up no farther, not unless she wanted to roast herself.

Riley didn't try bringing her own magic forth; it would only be a waste of time. She had to beat him with her steel.

The man swung his sword in an uppercut.

Riley stepped back, letting her feet go through a space in the ladder. His sword missed its target and swung upward as Riley grabbed a wooden beam. Riley swung *hard*, moving toward her ship and past her enemy. She hooked her legs on the ladder, then pulled herself up through another hole, giving her a separation of five feet from him.

She leapt, turning in mid-air and landing with her sword between the two of them.

The man's eyes were wide, clearly having seen nothing like that before.

"Impressed? Come get some, and I'll show you what else I can do."

She felt heat at her back again, this time from the other side of the ladder. He was going to force her to face him, and that was fine. Riley was ready.

His sword was a blur, but Riley rushed forward. She was a dancer, her partner her own sword and the tune they danced to was that of war.

She met each blow but didn't give ground. She pushed forward, ducking, sweeping with her leg while also slicing with her sword. The man parried, heading toward his ship's wall of flames. Riley pressed on, slamming her sword down—utilizing her strength now.

Wham! Wham! Wham!

For the first time she saw fear in the man's eyes; he realized that this warrior was unlike anyone he'd faced.

Fire erupted from his hands, but Riley gave him no time to fling it at her. She leapt and her feet snaked through the air, catching the man in his stomach. He doubled over, and Riley landed on his back. The ladder wobbled under them as she brought her sword down across his neck.

They were inches from the wall of flames. Riley smelled smoke rising into the air.

"*YIELD!*" she screamed. "*YIELD OR DIE!*"

There was true wonder in the man's eyes. True fear too.

"I yield," he said. The flames behind him went out. "I yield."

Breath raged in and out of Riley's lungs when she realized she wouldn't have to kill him. That he was actually *yielding*.

A roar went up from her ship—raucous cheers.

Riley backed up, the adrenaline fading from her body. She looked around, seeing where she was for the first time in long minutes. She stood between two ships over an ocean on a ladder.

She laughed, shaking her head. "Holy hell."

The red-haired woman was a few feet in front of her, also on the ladder. Riley's sword ripped into the air again, prepared to take whatever the woman was ready to give.

"No need, dear," Erin Stormhandle declared. "You won, and I honor my word. My ship and my crew are yours. Meet Eric Stormhandle, my son, and the only member of my crew."

Riley's eyes narrowed, and the woman laughed.

"Trust me, you'll like the ship."

Riley looked at the man on the other side of the ship's mess hall. Eric Stormhandle.

He was looking back at her, but his face wasn't as cold as it'd been above. He was still in awe of her, and Riley didn't know how to handle it.

He hadn't stopped staring at her since their fight had ended. Erin hadn't been lying about the two of them being the entirety of the crew. Verith and his soldiers had searched her ship level by level and hadn't found another soul.

"There's no need for more than us, not with a ship like that," she explained. "There's enough energy to do everything we need."

"You're pirates." William was standing at the mess hall's door as if he thought the two newcomers might rush out. "Your kind makes your life off raping and pillaging others. Ships like ours. Good people who venture too far out into this watery wilderness."

Erin smiled. Riley sensed no hatred from her, and no fear either. She wasn't angry that she no longer owned her ship, and she wasn't scared of anyone—as if she'd planned this, or had known it would come.

"That was just a...Well, 'bluff' might be the correct term. Eric and I do that because we have to, or at least we did in the beginning. It was important for us to instill fear in the rest of the pirates on the seas, especially when it got to be just the two of us."

"Hell, Stormhandle, you're gonna have to start makin' sense." William was not pleased with her answer.

Riley remained silent, wanting to listen before she made a decision. Lucie, Worth, and Verith were all in the mess hall, too. The fight outside had set up a division of labor that everyone seemed pleased with—Verith ran the ship, and Riley made decisions that affected the mission.

Erin was still smiling, William's displeasure not affecting her at all.

"Sure, sure. I'll explain since we're now part of your crew. Have you all heard of Irth?"

William only glared.

Riley shook her head. "We're from New Perth. We do not travel the great seas. We're content with what we have."

Erin's eyes narrowed, the smile disappearing. "Interesting. I've never met anyone from New Perth. Never even heard of it, but then again, this is the farthest we've ventured from our usual shores." She dropped the concerned look and smiled again. "My point is, where I'm from, certain places don't approve of magic or those who can use it."

"I know," Riley said. "New Perth has until recently been one of them."

"You don't use magic?"

Riley grinned. "We're coming around to it, perhaps by force. Tell us more about you, though."

"Well, a class of Paladins started persecuting all magic users, and we bolted. There used to be a lot of us on that ship. Ten. My whole family left our city because Eric could use magic and they wanted to kill him. The city thought it was a curse to be eradicated, so my family and I simply left. This was fifteen years ago or so."

She turned around and looked at her son.

"When Eric was just a little boy."

He remained quiet.

"The sea isn't an easy place, and we found that out quickly. Most pirate outfits don't last very long. He and I have lasted *much* longer than we should, but it's because of our tricks and his magic."

"What do you mean by tricks?" William asked.

"We haven't actually had to *meet* another pirate ship in quite some time, because we were smart in the beginning.

When we first began, we were ruthless. We had to be. Using Eric's magic and our sword training, we fended off a lot of attacks and killed a lot of people.

"The flag you see on our ship is well known among pirates now. They don't want anything to do with us, because they know our ship is more powerful than theirs. They run. You didn't, which was when I knew something was different."

"Like what?" William asked.

"Well, for one, we didn't recognize your flag. We knew you weren't pirates immediately. In this business, though, you have to be aggressive or you end up dead. Most of my family died over the years." Erin looked down at the table in front of her. "The sea isn't easy."

"Why didn't ya just find another city?" William asked. "One that likes magic?"

"Some people did. Not everyone died aboard our ship. Some left us when we went ashore, but I decided when I escaped the persecution that I wasn't subjecting Eric to that again. We would not be run out because of his talents. On the sea, we're a city to ourselves."

Riley leaned forward. "Then why are you here with us? If you don't want to be on land again in another city that might run you out, why did you surrender?"

The woman glanced at her son once more.

"Well, I didn't think we'd lose." She laughed. "Eric's never lost. He's the best swordsman I've ever seen, and when you combine that with the fire he produces, there hasn't been anyone who could best him. There's a certain finality to this life that you can't avoid, though. Perhaps if Eric had welched and run back to the ship, we could have withstood you. Our ship *is* powerful, more so than any other I've ever seen, but there's only two of us, and that matters."

"You were going to let your son die?" Riley asked.

"I wasn't born to life at sea, but it's something I adopted. I'm not lying to you when I say I'm the captain of that ship, and we are pirates. We're not as evil as some of them, but we understand the rules of warfare at sea."

She looked at Riley.

"You didn't kill him, though. You're not a pirate, and the bald man over there—I think he has some magic in him too, if I had to guess."

"Aye, Worth magic." He smiled as he spoke, his eyes saying he liked the woman on the other side of the table...and not just for her beauty.

Worth knew about being run out of cities, too. Maybe not for magic, but when you were unwanted, did the reason really matter?

"You let him live. If you hadn't, maybe I would have gone ahead and fought you too. I'm not as good with a sword and I don't have magic, but I'm decent with my blade, and my ship could blow yours to shreds. I might have lived. I might have died.

"But you let *him* live, so now I think we might have found a place where we can set down the pirate life. Where we can make ourselves at home. With you, with this New Perth kingdom, if you'll have us."

William groaned and looked at Riley. "First the mutants, now magical outcasts from across the Great Sea. Just let 'em take their ship and get the hell outta here."

Riley winked at the woman, then asked, "Worth, have you and your kind saved the rude man's ass?"

"Aye, betcha. Save many time." Worth grinned from ear to ear.

"Can you remind me who taught him magic?"

"Aye. Worth taught. Worth still teachin'. He hard-headed, though."

"That he is," Riley agreed. "So, William, the Prefect's Right Hand, do you not think these two can teach us a thing or two about the sea, and maybe a thing or two about magic?"

"He forgets how much he has to learn, doesn't he?" Lucie chimed in.

Everyone was grinning now—everyone but William. He continued looking *pissed* for a few seconds but finally started laughing.

"Fine, smartass. Bring these two on. I ain't responsible, though, if they steal all our stuff."

Riley turned to the woman and her son. "As Right Hand of Mason Ire, Assistant Prefect of New Perth, I welcome you as citizens. Your magic and your ship are welcome and will be treated with the respect they both deserve."

CHAPTER FIVE

"I'm growing bored, Artino."

Rendal watched the slight man walk around his makeshift laboratory.

"That's not my problem, Rendal. I have work to do. So much work, and you've brought me out here on the ocean where my beakers keep sliding and breaking. And look. Just look, Rendal. Right there."

Rendal did. A bunch of broken glass had been swept into the corner.

He smiled.

Artino was a genius, but damn if he wasn't neurotic.

"Those were some good-looking beakers, weren't they?"

Artino stopped moving around, unable to understand that Rendal was toying with him. He stared at the beakers, looking sad.

"They were. They really were."

Rendal stifled a laugh.

"Okay, Artino. Soon I'll get you all the beakers you

could possibly want. When we get to New Perth, I'm going to set you up with a whole floor of that damned castle full of nothing but beakers."

"What do you *want*, Rendal? I have work to do." The man stopped staring and went back to his workbench.

"I'm bored and there's work to be done, so I need to know how we can go about it?"

Artino shook his head. "*I* know there's work to be done. I wonder if *you* know it. What is it, Rendal? Get to the point, please, for the love of all that's holy."

Rendal smiled, knowing the man was reaching a breaking point. Rendal had to rein it in some, or the man might snap—and above all, that could *not* happen. Rendal needed his genius.

"I need more people, plain and simple. We have enough to battle those coming, but that's not what I'm preparing for. I'm going to turn the Right Hand, then we're going to attack New Perth. I have to assume they're building their defenses, and what I currently have isn't going to be enough."

"What's this have to do with me?"

Rendal wanted to throttle the little scientist, but he kept his temper in check as he said, "It has *everything* to do with you. You're the one who created this *technology* that's allowing me to do it all."

"Oh, Rendal, all your power, and you can be so dense sometimes."

"What are you talking about?" Rendal asked.

The scientist didn't look at him as he opened one of the red necklaces.

"You know what the green necklaces do, right?"

Rendal nodded. "Yes. They create confusion among the nanocytes so that they can't focus on the user's directions."

"Partly correct." He shook his head. "It amazes me how little you understand about all this."

"Well, enlighten me, then."

"I'm afraid if I tell you it'll ruin everything." Artino quit fooling with the necklace. "I know what will happen if it does."

"What's that?"

"Given our current location, I imagine I'll be shark food before the night is over."

"Oh, Artino." Rendal moved across the room and sat down on a chair. He swung his feet up on the table. "There's nothing you could tell me that would make me hurt you. You're safe with me, probably more than anyone else in this world. Now, friend, tell me what I'm not understanding."

The scientist sighed, clearly knowing he had no choice. "*Some* of the technology is because of me. Draining the nanocytes and uniting them with your blood—that's technology powered by amphoralds. I invented the tech to make that possible, true enough. The necklaces that create confusion among the nanocytes, limiting a magic user's ability, that's my tech, too."

"So what am I missing?"

"The army you're creating. That isn't technology, or… not completely."

Rendal grew very still. "Be careful here, Artino. I don't suffer liars well."

"I'm not lying! I have *never* lied to you! You've never asked about any of this, just trusted me!" The scientist whipped around so that he was looking at Rendal, his eyes wide and sweat on his brow.

Rendal smiled broadly. "Just kidding, Artino. You're safe. No worries. Now finish."

"I don't want to."

"Hey, Artino, is it going to stop me from doing what I want to do?"

"It may."

Rendal's eyes turned red, and he waved his fingers toward his chest. Artino floated slowly into the air, listening to his command.

"You don't have a choice in the matter, Artino. I hate to break it to you, but you don't. Now tell me."

"The red necklaces. The red bracelet." The man's words flew from his mouth, running together, his fear great. "They're focus mechanisms. They keep the magic user from using their own magic, but they allow you to focus harder than you usually would. They allow you to control the subject's mind at a much deeper level."

Rendal put his hand down, and Artino fell to the floor. He was shaking.

"Calm down, Artino. Calm down. You're fine." Rendal dropped his feet to the floor and swiveled his chair around so that his back was to the scientist. "So it's not technology that's allowing me to use them, it's mind control?"

"Yes and no. The technology is keeping *them* from using their magic, keeping their nanocytes from following their directions. But when you step in and command them to do something, the bracelets and necklaces light up and their nanocytes listen to *you*, not the host. Well, that's not completely correct either. The nanocytes *are* listening to the host, but the host is listening to you. Does that make sense?"

"It's my magic that's making this work?" Rendal asked.

"Yes. The number of nanocytes in your bloodstream is higher than any concentration I've ever seen. You can control entire armies, but you need focus objects and a way to scatter the nanocytes until you're ready."

"So I don't have to go to Sidnie? I can take people from anywhere? I don't have to take people who already use magic?" Rendal asked.

"Yes. Anyone will work since everyone has nanocytes in their bloodstream."

Rendal smiled. "Why were you nervous, Artino? This is great news. You're telling me I'm more powerful than I originally thought. There's no downside here."

"Th-Th-That's not true," Artino stumbled out. "It might have been a placebo. You thought it worked because you were convinced of the technology. Now that you know it really rests inside you, maybe it won't work anymore."

Rendal spun the chair around again. "Nonsense, Artino. The technology is there. This is actually a great gift. Do you have any idea how many pirate ships are on these seas? I can gather an armada just by floating around."

Artino nodded quickly. "Yes, that's one way to look at it."

Rendal clapped his hands together and stood up. "Great news! Now, tell me what else you're working on. You know I don't like complacency, Artino."

The fear drained from the scientist as he thought about his work again.

He walked back to the desk he was working at.

"I'm working with the amphoralds, Rendal. I'm trying to engineer weapons that won't rely just on your magical abilities but can also tie into them."

"Oh, Artino, you know the way to my heart, my dear friend. Please, please, tell me more."

"Harold, I had an idea earlier in the day."

Rendal lay on the upper deck. His chest was bare, and he was letting the sun tan his skin. He'd been working hard for a long, long time, and soon more hard work would arrive, so he was taking a few moments to enjoy himself.

"Yes, sir," Harold responded. "How can I help?"

"Well, first, look at Mason over there. Excuse me, *Assistant Prefect* Mason. I want to make sure I'm using his proper title." Rendal winked at Mason, who was leaning against one of the ship's railings. He was dressed in the same clothes he'd been captured in, although they were dirty and holey now. "I asked him to join me in sunbathing, and he's resolutely refusing. Can you believe that?"

The Assistant Prefect refused to look over.

"It seems foolish to me, sir," Harold answered.

"Yes, yes, to me as well. No matter. I learned long ago that my happiness can't be tied to someone else's. If he wants to be a sourpuss, I suppose I have to let him. Come, sit, Harold. Let's discuss my idea."

Harold moved across the deck and grabbed a wooden stool. He put it next to Rendal's chair and sat.

"We're in infested waters, Harold. Do you realize that?"

"With sharks?"

"With pirates. They're everywhere. If I send my mind out even a little way, I can pick up ten ships. They're like vultures looking for something weak or dying."

"I don't understand, sir. I don't think we have to worry about pirates, given what happened a few days ago."

"I'm not *worried* about them, Harold. I *want* them."

Harold's eyes narrowed. "I'm still not understanding, sir."

"We're going to New Perth soon. We're going to show up and take the kingdom over. You're with me that far, right?"

Harold nodded.

"We need more people. I want to take no possible chance that New Perth can repel us. I think we have a whole ocean full of killers, and I think it might be a good idea to enlist them."

Rendal saw realization dawn in Harold's eyes.

"How do we do it, though? How would we get to them?"

Rendal reached forward and slapped Harold's knee, laughing. "You still don't have a lot of faith! I've got an idea for that too!" He looked at Mason. "Tell him, Assistant Prefect. You and I were just talking about it, weren't we?"

"He's a lunatic," Mason retorted, "and so are you for following him."

"Ha!" Rendal sat up, laughing. "I love this guy. Always with the insults! Come on, Mason. Tell Harold what we discussed!"

Mason sighed and shook his head. "He's going to throw up a distress signal. A firework."

"Exactly. It'll bring them to us like a dead carcass brings vultures. From *miles* around, Mason."

"Sir, please don't think I doubt you, but if we bring ten ships full of pirates, will we be able to handle them?"

Rendal nodded, smiling. "Oh, yes. That won't be a problem. By the end of the next few days, you're going to be running an armada, Harold."

"Yes, sir."

"Okay," Rendal said. "That's all I needed you for. We'll meet tonight about the distress signal."

Harold stood. "Thank you, sir."

Rendal's second-in-command walked off.

"You'll never be able to rule New Perth." Mason scoffed.

Rendal looked at him. The young man was staring into the distance, watching the endless ocean slowly toss and turn.

"Why would you say such a harsh thing, Mason? I should have been the first ruler, but I was robbed of that opportunity. I personally think I'll make a fine Prefect." Rendal wore a sly grin.

"You rule this ship by fear. You rule that crew of zombie-like creatures with necklaces. My father doesn't rule like that, and neither did my grandfather—"

"Don't you mention that man in front of me," Rendal snapped. "Don't even say his name."

Mason smiled now, turning from the sea to the mage. "Simon?"

Rendal's eyes turned red, but Mason didn't look away.

"Your magic doesn't scare me, Rendal. The fear tactics you rule this ship with won't work on me. You can kill me. You can toss me right over the rail, and it won't matter. Riley is coming, and that means you're going to die. I don't care about the armada you're building or the group of people you control with magic. Riley is stronger than them all, and when she kills you, I'll be the one laughing."

The mage's eyes faded. "You're as foolish as your grandfather. He's dead, and I'm alive. I promise you, young Prefect, the same will happen to you."

"You're a silly, insane old man. You don't even know the storm that's coming for you," Mason answered as he looked back at the sea.

CHAPTER SIX

"Ale. That's all I give a damn about," William remarked.

"The island isn't that big, chubby," Riley told him. "I think you'll be able to find it pretty easily."

Erin stepped up next to Riley. She'd directed them to this small island, something they never would have found on their own. "There's a bar down to our right. We could all go there and talk a bit if you like?"

"They have ale?" William asked.

"It's a bar, dummy. Of course they have ale," Lucie taunted.

William grumbled something that Riley couldn't hear and started walking before anyone could retort.

Erin remained next to Riley, her son Eric slightly behind both of them. Lucie was on Riley's other side as Worth picked up his pace to get to the alehouse at the same time as William.

Riley smiled.

"Ocean's End is a dangerous place," Erin said. "Only

pirates know about it, and there isn't any truce when you land here. What keeps the peace is that every single person who shows up is tough as hell, and they'll all kill at the drop of a hat."

"So it's a safe place, is what you're saying?" Riley joked.

"Something like that." Erin smirked. "Verith, what did you think of the ship?"

Verith was behind them, walking ahead of a group of the soldiers he had picked to accompany them off the ship.

"It's amazing. I'm not sure I understand it yet, but it's going to give us firepower we couldn't imagine before. How did you get it? The ship, I mean?"

"We built it," Erin answered happily. "It took us a long time and we did a lot of trading, but we lined the ship with the stones. They call them 'amphoralds' where I'm from. The ship doesn't rely on the wind; it's powered by energy stored in the green gems. That's what the amphoralds do, basically—they hold energy that the ship can use a lot of different ways."

"Where's their energy come from?" Verith asked.

"From us!" Erin smiled.

Riley liked the woman. A pirate and a cutthroat, maybe, but her humor was infectious.

"Humans power the amphoralds, so as long as we're alive, the amphoralds will be too."

"That's amazing." Verith seemed lost in thought.

"We picked up the idea from Arcadia and the surrounding cities."

The group reached the alehouse. The island was small, only about two miles in diameter. Erin said it was strictly used by pirates, but it enjoyed a brisk business because of how many ships patrolled the seas.

Riley stepped inside the alehouse.

It was a dingy thing with low lighting. The tables were scattered haphazardly around the building, and the bar had been carved up by knives. It looked like anyone who'd ever sat at the bar had thought it their duty to carve a new symbol or slogan into it.

The bartender glanced up, one eyebrow rising at this new group.

"They know you're not pirates, but keeping moving." Erin grabbed Riley's elbow surreptitiously and pulled her forward.

"What gives that away? The giant up ahead wearing a purple robe?"

"Yeah, might be. Or the crew of armor-clad soldiers behind you." Erin grinned as if this were the most fun she'd had in years.

"This'll do just fine." William pulled out a chair from a large round table and sat down. "Now I want to drink in peace, all of youse. Don't aggravate me with nonsense like you do on the ship."

Riley sat down next to him and leaned in close. "Remember, we're all about saving Mason. This is a momentary break."

"Aye, I know, Right Hand. Let me play my part of boisterous prick and I'll let you play yours of concerned servant, then both of us can get to the business of kickin' Rendal's ass."

Riley smiled and leaned away from her partner in crime.

"WHADDAYA HAVE?" The bartender didn't move from behind the bar as he called for their orders.

"ALE!" William shouted.

"WINE!" Worth shouted at the exact same time.

The two big men looked at each other and started laughing.

The group was large, about twenty people, and they took up the entire table plus a smaller one next to it.

"Right Hand," Erin said. "I have a request of you."

"Sure, what is it?"

"Would you work with my son on his swordsmanship? I've taught him everything I can, but I can't teach him the things you can. If you teach him, he and I will both become your loyal subjects. We'll be *your* Right Hands."

William laughed. "Oh, this is rich! Riley don't need no Right Hands. She's got two left feet as it is; was barely able to hop around on that ladder. I'll teach the young lad everything he needs to know about a sword, then you two can serve me."

"Hush, fool," Lucie scoffed. "No one's ever walked across a ladder like her before. Your fat ass would have been shark food."

Riley ignored them both, looking at Erin. "I'll teach him what I can, but I can't accept your fealty. I serve the Kingdom, and Mason specifically. A Right Hand has no Right Hands. We have no servants. *We* serve."

"You'll have our loyalty, all the same."

Riley looked at Eric. "You want to learn more?"

He nodded. The death-filled look she'd seen on the ladder was gone. He looked like little more than a kid now, a twenty-year-old who probably didn't really know how much his life was going to change.

The world he'd known was gone, and he no longer had to be the protector of his mother and himself.

He looks lost, Riley thought, then, *So I'll help him find himself, the same way Lucie did for me.*

"I'll teach you, Eric," she told him. "I must say, though, you're no slouch. I imagine you'll teach me a few things too."

Eric smiled slightly at that.

The ale and wine showed up. William and Worth poured first, not even glancing at anyone else.

"They're savages." Lucie grinned.

"Aye, mayhap, but you'll be thankful for these savages when wolves show up at the door."

"They may just have come in," Erin whispered.

Riley's eyes were already on the people entering the alehouse. Her senses were attuned to everything in this place, and the moment new people pushed through the swinging doors, she focused on them.

"Who are they?" she asked without moving her lips, her voice floating to Erin without anyone else hearing.

"There's a loose-knit group of pirates that flies under one flag. Most ships follow their own captain, but there's a group that's trying to get economies of scale, basically. They all follow a man named Captain Johnny Twocuts. Those two men there wear Twocuts insignia."

Riley saw the patches on their shoulders—black fabric with two long red knife wounds overlaying it.

"Twocuts?" she asked.

"Yes. He's had his throat slit twice."

Riley looked at her, eyebrows raised.

"I'm not lying. It's why he's been able to get so many ships to fly his banners. He's a tough sonofabitch."

"And now they're looking at us," Riley commented.

The two men sat down at the bar, and more came in behind them—the entire ship was emptying into the alehouse, apparently. The two leaders were staring at Riley and the other women at the table.

"We about to have some trouble, skinny?" William took a deep sip of his beer, acting like he hadn't asked anything.

"I think so."

"Most definitely," Erin answered. "They sense blood in the water. They think we're weak, regardless of the armor your men are wearing."

Sure enough, the first two men stood up. Each held a large metal mug full of booze, and they walked over to Riley's table.

"Aye, whose flag ya fly?" the one on the right asked. He wore a large gold hoop earring in his right ear, and his front tooth was a dead yellow.

"Worth flag." The tent man smiled, his lips already slightly purple. "You like?"

"Never heard of it," the one on the left responded. "Don't think there is no Worth flag. Aye, I think ye might be lyin' to us."

"Aye." Worth picked up his cup and drank deeply. "Mayhap."

Riley saw that Worth's eyes weren't red yet. He was just joking around with these pirates.

William put his ale down heavily, amber liquid sloshing

over the sides of the cup. "Me and my friends here are trying to drink in peace. Can we help you two?"

"Ha!" The one on the left looked at his partner. "Can they help us? That's nice, ain't it? Can *they* help *us?*"

"Aye, that is nice." The pirate took a step closer to the table, slipping a knife from his belt. He moved it easily and with obvious skill as he slammed it into the table and pulled his hand back. It vibrated and swayed, but remained standing. "I think ya can help us. I think the redhead there is Stormhandle, and if she's shackin' up with the likes o' landlubbers, then she ain't no pirate no more. That 'bout right, Stormhandle?"

Erin flashed a brilliant grin. "Could be. I always said you should get out when you're on top. Given that none of you could do anything to me for twenty years, I figure it's time to retire."

"Mayhap that's true, mayhap it ain't. Either way, even if you're a landlubber now, that ship of yours belongs to the sea. Since I'm here, I say it belongs to Twocuts and me."

Erin didn't drop her smile. "Belongs to the sea? That's not how the law works, and you know it. It belongs to me so long as I can hold it, and if I'm with these landlubbers, then it belongs to them so long as they can hold it. No law says a landlubber can't hold a ship. You two are just over here jabbering your jaws, so let us drink."

Riley's hands were on the table, but she knew she could move quickly enough to slice both their throats before they'd be able to grab their dicks, let alone a weapon.

The pirates turned to William, thinking his size made him the leader. "Aye, think you can hold that ship from us?"

"I'd have a tougher time holding this ale down, truth be

told. You two are lower than whale shit, and if you don't know, that's at the bottom of your beloved ocean." He looked at Riley. "You had enough of this yet?"

"Don't look at yer wife, fat man," the pirate scolded. "Look at *me* when I'm talkin' to ya."

"Yes, I've had enough." Riley gritted her teeth.

She leapt to her feet, pushing her from the chair onto the table. Ale and wine spilled, with Worth shouting, "*NO!*"—apparently more worried about his beverage than the fight they were all facing.

Riley's sword was already out, and the tip touched the first pirate's forehead. "Come try to take the ship from us, although I imagine you'll only be taking my steel through your skull."

The entire alehouse was up and holding their weapons, everyone staring at this beyond-fast woman and the pirate who had challenged her.

"Did you think I sided with them because I had a choice?" Erin asked, still smiling. "I sided with them because they won."

Riley watched as Eric moved around the table. It was like watching herself, just younger. His feet moved like a ghost's, and his knife appeared from nowhere. He went behind the second pirate and put his knife across the man's throat.

"Meet my friend. His name's Eric."

Worth's eyes were red, and the wine and glasses that had spilled across the table were now floating in the air. "You spill wine."

"Hey, William? Were you planning on doing anything besides watching us?" Riley asked.

William remained sitting, his mug almost full. He took a drink. "You can handle my light work."

Riley's eyes focused again on the pirate. "What's it going to be?"

"Ye *are* a landlubber if you think there's any way you're walking out of this. Get her, boys!"

Riley looked up just in time.

A knife was flipping end over end directly for her. She moved her shoulder to the right, dodging the blade. The pirate beneath her had moved, but Worth was already fighting.

The chalices and mugs flew outward at frightening speed and slammed into pirates' heads, dropping them cold.

Riley jumped from the table, striking someone in the head with her foot as she did. The man fell to the ground, blood leaking from his ears. She started on the rest, her sword cutting through attackers like a shark through water. She saw everything and nothing at once, her mind focused on killing. She ran her sword across stomachs and backs alike, people dropping around her as if they'd never lived at all.

William didn't move from the table, just sat there smiling and drinking his ale.

Cries filled the air, and metal struck at Riley. She parried and sliced, ducked and kicked.

Objects were flying about, which was Worth's handiwork. He still stood by William, using his magic to help her. Verith's men were fighting as well, although they were far less capable than Riley.

She caught glimpses of Eric as she attacked. He fought

with a mixture of William's brutal strength and her lightning speed, a battering ram of quickness. He'd donned his face of death again, seeing these pirates as things to be dispatched.

As she spun around an attacker, Riley's heart froze.

Somehow a pirate had made his way behind William. The damn giant was enjoying watching this fight too much to notice, content to sip his ale and do nothing.

Riley couldn't make it in time.

She couldn't save him.

The pirate pulled a curved blade.

Riley didn't think.

She didn't have time.

She launched her sword, having no idea her eyes had turned bright red.

The sword didn't fly end over end but shot straight like an arrow—somehow *increasing* its speed.

Riley stared at her target.

The pirate's curved blade reached William's neck, ready to rip it wide open.

Riley's sword plunged into the pirate's forehead, cracking the bone and splitting his skull. It drove him back, then went through the wall and pinning him to it.

The sword burst into flames, which spread over the man's face.

William sat with his mouth open, his mug halfway between the table and his lips.

The cries around Riley had faded. The pirates were either losing interest or dying.

"Told you." Worth was smiling broadly, his lips now a deeper purple. "She magic."

"I don't know how I did it," Riley mused. "I didn't *control* it. It just happened, just like at Rendal's compound."

The four people surrounding Riley could all use magic at will—Worth, William, Lucie, and now Eric.

The alehouse had emptied quickly, the rest of the pirates deciding they wanted no part of the mage warriors. The dead pirates were being dragged outside by the employees.

No one stared at the newcomers now.

No one wanted anything to do with this crew.

"She magic." Worth nodded, his entire mouth purple. He wasn't full-on drunk yet, but he was getting close.

William just looked at him. "You're gonna be worthless on the ship. Too drunk to be of any use."

"'Cept with magic. Then Worth useful."

They all laughed as the bald man drank more from his chalice.

Erin had gone outside the alehouse with Verith and the soldiers. She said she couldn't use magic, so there was no sense staying inside with the rest of them.

"What did it feel like?" Lucie asked from across the table.

Riley closed her eyes, remembering the battle. "I just knew he was in trouble. William. I knew he was going to die and that I couldn't get to him in time. If I didn't do *something*, he'd die."

"Well, that's bullshit." William grinned as he looked around the table. "I had that pirate, no problem."

Riley opened her eyes. "Was that why you were sitting there with a beer in your hand?"

"Exactly. Was just waiting for the right moment."

Riley rolled her eyes and looked back at Lucie. "I guess I felt pressure. A lot of it. And that was the same thing I felt with Rendal—immense pressure."

"That's what allows me to cast fire," Eric interjected. He'd only spoken a handful of times, and not at all since the skirmish ended.

Riley looked at him. "What do you mean?"

"I can't do it right now."

Everyone at the table looked at him. Even Worth, who was grinning wildly.

"Say what?" William asked.

Eric nodded. "I can't. I can only cast when I'm fighting. The pressure… That's what allows me to do it. I've never met anyone else like that."

"You haven't been able to fix it? So that you can cast right now?" Riley asked.

He shook his head. "No. I have to feel… I don't know, like I or someone else might die."

William spoke up. "That's not good. We need you able to kick ass all the time, not just when I'm acting like I might get hurt."

"You're a pretty good actor." Lucie chuckled.

"I know. I should get an award for it. I'm good enough that I suppose I could act like I'm always about to die, but that would severely cut down on the number of men I'm able to kill." William grinned broadly.

Riley shook her head, looking at the table. "I've got to

get a handle on this if I'm going to beat Rendal. I can't be useful only when people are about to die."

"Or *acting* like they're about to die." William laughed.

"Hush your mouth, fool," Lucie chastised. She looked at Riley. "There's time yet, girl. We're not to him. You'll be fine."

"Tough student." Worth's smile fell away. "Tough-headed. No listen."

He stood up, grabbed his chalice, and walked away from the table.

"What the hell is his problem?" Riley asked, feeling anger at Worth for the first time.

William smiled. "You're just not as good a student as I am, and it's buggin' him."

"Shut it," Riley answered.

"Rendal isn't blocking himself from me, Riley," Lucie told her. "I can see where he's at, and we're another week away. We'll get you using magic by then."

"And if not, I'll put the team on my back and carry us." William laughed again. "Like I always do."

Riley shot him a glare but said nothing. It was clear she was growing angry and was not in the mood for his jokes.

"Hey." William's smile faded. "You did good, skinny. You did real good. All jokes aside, you saved my bacon, and I'm embarrassed about how many times you keep doing it. Don't worry about the magic; you'll get there."

Riley nodded, her glare disappearing. "Thank you."

The ale house's door opened. William, Riley, and Eric were all on their feet at once, weapons brandished.

"Calm yourselves, my friends. I'm not the one to kill." It

was Erin, still beaming her devilish smile. "But we do have more trouble."

"Of course we do," William groaned. "Ever since Pat showed up talkin' about Rendal, we've had nothin' but trouble."

"Come on out here. You'll want to hear this."

The crew stood and made their way outside, William taking the lead and Riley walking behind him. She was still in her thoughts, unsure about the confidence everyone else felt in her. Everyone but Worth.

Maybe he was right.

Maybe she *was* too stubborn.

They stepped outside and Riley could hear the ocean in the distance, a constant presence on this island.

Verith's soldiers had spread around the porch, creating a barrier between those inside and anyone who might want to enter. Verith stood at attention.

A pirate was on his right. He wore the Twocuts insignia, but he wasn't brandishing a weapon.

"Twocuts is requesting our presence," Erin told the group as they reached the porch.

"I'm sure he is," William retorted. "We just killed all his men, and I killed *at least* ten of them by myself. Sure he wants to see me front and center."

Worth laughed. "You kill like you drink. Weak."

William's head snapped to the bald man. "Watch it."

"Watch you drink one beer. Take all day." Worth grinned broadly.

"Boys, can we stay focused for just a moment?" Erin asked. "You can measure dicks or beer or whatever later. Right now, Twocuts wants to see us."

"What if we don't want to see him?" Riley answered. "We don't have time to be meeting people; we've got to get to Mason."

"Yes, I know. However, there does seem to be a problem with that, which is what I mentioned inside. You see, Twocuts has about twenty ships around the island. Inside the bar, we can defeat them, but even if we pull all Verith's men off the ship, we're still vastly outnumbered."

"Why the hell did we come here?" William asked angrily.

"You seemed fine with it when you wanted beer," Lucie said.

"Well I've had my beer, and now I'm wondering *why*?"

"It doesn't matter." Riley stepped forward and looked at the pirate. "What does your captain want?"

"Parley."

"You believe him?" Riley asked Erin.

"On the seas, if a captain requests parley, you're guaranteed safety. If Twocuts was to break that rule, he'd be in an awful lot of trouble with every other captain on the sea."

"Then why can't we just leave?" William grumbled. "If he wants to parley and we don't, we can just walk away."

The pirate shook his head. "Landlubbers."

"That's not how it works. If he requests parley and we decline, there's nothing keeping him from attacking us," Erin told them.

Riley nodded. "So we accept or risk war."

"Exactly," Erin answered.

"Well, not much of a choice then. Verith, your men ready?" Riley called down the steps.

"Yes. Do you trust this parley, Erin?"

"I do."

Verith nodded. "Then I'll leave the rest of the men on our ships."

The crew walked across the island, the trip taking about thirty minutes. Riley was quiet as she walked, thinking about her magic use.

She remembered it much more clearly than she had at Rendal's compound.

She could still see the sword flying through the air, *knowing* she had complete control over it. She'd told it to go faster, and it had listened. She'd told it to hit the pirate's face, and it had.

She'd told it to make sure the man died for certain, and the blade had burst into flames.

The blade she carried on her side.

Yet, she had no idea how to do it again, and Eric had said he had the same problem. Only, he still had more control than she did. He could do more things as soon as a fight started.

Worth stepped up next to her. "Sword good, aye?"

She came out of her thoughts and looked at him. Worth was back to grinning, the chalice gone from his hand.

"Yeah, it is, Worth. It's the best sword I've ever had."

"It magic."

"You keep saying that, but then you also say *I'm* magic."

"Cannot both be magic?" Worth asked.

"I don't know." Riley shook her head. "I don't understand any of it."

Worth nodded. "You will. You magic. William!" Worth started jogging, leaving Riley and catching up with the other Right Hand.

She watched him go, truly not understanding what the man was talking about.

They finally reached the pirate ship. It was a massive thing, almost a city unto itself. Riley stared up in awe, understanding that the captain might have a lot of ships at his beck and call, but the loot mostly flowed one way—to this ship.

The pirate who had led them here had already gone aboard. William was the first of their crew to reach the ship.

Riley stepped up next to him.

"What do you think?" he asked.

"I think this thing is fucking huge."

"No, skinny. About the woman."

"Erin?" Riley's voice lowered.

"Yeah. You think I got a shot with her?" William whispered.

Riley couldn't keep the grin off her face. "You're serious right now? We're about to climb onto this huge pirate ship and meet a man who's had his throat slit twice, and you're worried about a date with *our* newly acquired *pirate*?"

"Zip it," William retorted. "Whaddaya think? I got a shot?'

Riley shook her head, still chuckling. The rest of the group was coming closer. "I think you'll have to play your cards right. You don't come off as the nicest man in the world."

"But I'm definitely the most handsome." He winked.

The pirate came back to the ship's main door. "Come aboard and follow me. The captain is in his chambers. Only you six. The soldiers and their leader stay outside."

"Fuck that!" William shouted.

Erin stepped next to him, putting her hand on his elbow. "It's fine. This is normal protocol. They won't hurt us."

William flinched at her touch; Riley had never seen anything like it from the big man.

He looked back at Riley. "What do you think?"

"I think we don't have much choice."

William grumbled something unintelligible.

Riley turned back to Verith. "Stand guard here, okay?"

"Of course," he answered. He seemed unperturbed, trusting the parley. Riley supposed that was because he knew more about it than she did, meaning Erin wasn't lying to them.

"I'll stay here too," Lucie told them.

"Why?" Riley asked.

"If Worth goes in there, it'll be helpful to have someone outside who knows magic."

Riley nodded; Lucie was right. She gazed at the red-haired woman. "We've just met, Erin, but we're putting a lot of trust in you. You understand that?"

Erin looked at her, the smile gone. "I know. My son and I were looking for a home. I think we've found it with you. You accept him, and that's the most important thing. I only wish the rest of my family had made it long enough to see this. I'm not leading you astray. I think Twocuts will treat us fairly."

Riley nodded and turned to William. "All right, chubby, you ready?"

"I liked things better when I was in charge."

"Hell, *I* liked it better, too," Riley answered. "You want to be in charge?"

"No." William grinned. "If you die and I have to tell Mason, I want to say you're the one who put us on the ship."

"Ha. Ha. Ha." Riley looked up at the pirate waiting for them. "Let's go."

The crew walked up the gangplank, Riley leading the way. William came next, then Erin, her son, and finally the purple-mouthed Worth.

"No magic here," Worth told everyone.

For all his drinking and jolliness, Riley understood that he might be the most dangerous of all of them.

They entered the ship and wound their way through wooden passages.

"Erin, have you seen Twocut before?" Riley asked.

"No. His ships stayed away from ours. The man is smart, which is how he's gotten so many people under his banner. He would have lost against us, so he never challenged us."

"You were pretty smart, too," William commented. "You managed to make an entire community think you had more than two of you on board."

Riley smiled, knowing what a compliment from William meant—even if sounded stilted as hell.

The pirate stopped and turned around. "This here is the captain's quarters. I need not mention that very few people are allowed inside, and that yer here under the rules of parley. That means ain't to be no fightin'. Ain't to be no killin'. Ain't to be no magic or whatever the hell y'all used in that alehouse. Ya understand?"

"We gotcha, pirate man," William bellowed. "Now get outta the way and let us meet this damned captain."

The pirate sneered, but he knew his place. He pulled no weapons, and wouldn't break the sea's code.

He turned around and opened the door, his voice louder as he spoke. "Captain Twocuts, I present those ya requested."

Riley almost laughed at the man, who was trying to sound proper but was unable to do it correctly.

The pirate stepped through and Riley followed, the rest of the group entering and forming a line to her left and right—leaving Riley in the center.

The man in front of them was at the end of a long fur rug. Riley had never seen anything quite like it and had no idea what type of animal it was from.

The captain sat on a huge wooden chair, which was stained black. He wore black too, although Riley found it tough to decipher *what* he was wearing. Pants, a vest, and a shirt, but it looked like more. Somehow the clothes covered almost every part of him, including gloves on his hands. All of it black.

His hair was long and he wore it in braids, which fell around his face. His skin was deeply tanned, and his eyes were set deep.

The two scars across his throat were pronounced; much whiter than the rest of his skin.

"Aye, those I requested," the captain said. "I suppose he ain't bother gettin' yer names, aye? The pretty blonde, there—what do ya call yerself?"

"Riley Trident, Right Hand of Assistant Prefect Mason Ire, loyal servant of New Perth's kingdom."

"A long name, aye. I take it ye know who I am."

"We've heard," Riley answered.

"No doubt from the redheaded bitch standing at yer side." The captain said it with a smile, and Riley saw Erin match it with one of her own. "Aye, don't take that too personally, Riley Trident, Right Hand of Such and Such. On the seas, we judge a person by their strength. We'll rape, kill, and steal from the weak, but the one next to ya don't count in that. I call her a bitch the same as I would a man."

"Why did you ask us here?" William interjected.

"Well, ya carved up a few of my pirates, from what I can tell. And that's fine. The strong survive on the sea, and ye all are mayhaps pretty strong. But ya don't belong here, that much is clear."

"I belong where I say I belong." William's voice grew louder.

"Aye, we got a live one, don't we?" Twocuts smiled. "We can keep this civil. Indeed, we best, as we are operatin' under certain rules."

"What William is asking," Riley said, "is why parley with us? Your men threatened us, and they lost. From what Erin says—"

"Erin?" the captain interrupted. "That's the fierce Stormhandle's name?"

"There was a reason you never attacked us." Eric spoke for the first time, and his voice was icy. "Don't forget that, Captain Twocuts."

The pirate laughed loudly, though without menace. "And the dangerous son. Well met, lad. Please continue, Right Hand, loyal servant of Such and Such."

Riley rolled her eyes at the slight but didn't let her anger rise. "From what *Captain Stormhandle* says such action as we took is accepted here, so William and I are trying to understand why you called this parley."

"You don't belong on the sea." The pirate looked at William. "I don't mean any offense, big man. Them's the facts, though. Y'all belong on land, but I find you out here on the sea, and it makes me wonder: what could make landlubbers venture out to dangerous waters? We've seen your ship. We saw your ship take Stormhandle's. We stayed away because my crew is smart, and there are other things brewin' on those seas."

The captain dropped all pretense of levity. This was the cutthroat Riley had expected.

"I'm wonderin' if what's brewin' a bit away from here has anything to do with you?"

Riley wasn't going to lie to the man. "We're chasing an outlaw mage. That's why we're on the seas. We came across Erin Stormhandle and had no choice but to fight. Same when we came here. Trouble keeps finding us, but our path is true. We're here to find an outlaw mage."

She *wouldn't* mention Mason's kidnapping. No one needed to know there was other valuable cargo aboard Rendal's ship.

"Aye, I thought that might be the case. Or at least you were out here after someone new. I don't know nothin' bout no mages, although I hear Stormhandle's boy there can light himself on fire and such. That true?"

Eric said nothing. Erin was quiet as well.

"Never mind. A ship broke apart days ago. Just completely crumbled into the water. Some of my ships found the survivors. They were floatin' in the sea, survivin' by holdin' onto pieces of wood that hadn't got waterlogged yet. Some of 'em didn't make it, of course, as things tend to go on the sea."

The captain gave a sickly grin, leaving no doubt in Riley's mind that his men had killed many—probably for sport.

"But the ones who did survive said something' about a mage. Some of 'em called him a magician. I don't know the difference, if there is one. But they said a man broke the ship with his hand, which I don't get even now. I didn't believe it then. Said he had an army of magicians, too. I didn't believe that either until I heard you all were causing a ruckus down at the alehouse. Now I wonder."

"He broke a ship with his hand?" Riley didn't see how that was possible either.

"That's what they said."

Worth nodded. "Magic. Not use hand. Use mind."

The captain turned to the bald man, his eyes wide at Worth's speech.

"If he says it, it's true," Riley responded.

"You're a magician?" the captain asked.

"I magic," Worth answered.

The captain sighed. "You are a weird lot, and that's sayin' somethin' given everythin' I've seen. There's more, though. We have eyes on the ship. I keep eyes on everything out here on the seas, much as I can anyway. Two nights ago it sent up a distress signal."

He smiled.

"My men ain't as dumb as some of the other ships out here. They said those other pirates went streakin' 'cross the water like water snakes. And ya know what happened when two of 'em got there?"

Riley's palms were sweating. "What?"

"Nothin'." Twocuts' smile widened. "Absolutely nothin'."

"Nothin' is what's between your ears, Captain Numbnuts," William said and turned to Riley. "Look. I've heard enough. Whether or not Rendal had some ships stop by his and not fight him, it don't matter, does it? We need to find him; that's all that matters."

"You're not listenin', landlubber," the captain sneered. "Pirate ships don't head to a distress call and then just *stop*. My men didn't go because they'd been watching this ship for a while, and they knew somethin' wasn't right 'bout it. Those other ships were dumb, but they should have sunk that ship after stealin' all its treasure, ya understand? The two ships *didn't*. They *joined* it."

William turned around. "What do ya mean?"

"They ain't flyin' no banners, but they're floating with it. That was two days ago. Now, I *kept* my ship on it, an' I got little speed ships goin' back and forth between this main ship and my others all the time. I wanted to know what was happenin'. Do *you* want to know, or you still got a hard dick to get out of here?"

William grunted, nodding his reluctant assent.

"Last night, a ship got too close to the three. I don't mean close in that it should have been in any danger, but still...too close, apparently. It moseyed its way into your magician's path, and now *it's* joined them too. That ain't normal. That ain't natural. And this magician's ship—if that's what he is—is heading south. Heading toward us, best I can tell."

Riley turned to Worth. "What's it mean?"

Worth was smiling and looking at William. "He got big head, aye?"

"Go fuck yourself, tent man." William tried to sound mad, but he couldn't hide his grin.

"Seriously, Worth, quit playing around. What does that mean, what the pirate said?"

"Aye, means mage is magic," Worth told them.

"I know *that*, but what about the ships?" Riley asked.

Worth chuckled. "He control minds. Ships now his. Men on ships now his. All his."

William's eyebrows got close together, and his expression grew concerned. "That's not possible. How many men are on a ship, Erin?"

"Anywhere from two to two hundred."

"We've got four hundred right here beneath us," Twocuts interjected.

"So he's got up to six hundred more people right now?" Riley asked.

"Aye, that's what I'm tryin' to tell ya, landlubbers. Your magician is getting an army together, and now he's headin' here. That means he's comin' to the island to gather the rest."

"How strong would he have to be to do that, Worth?"

Worth only shook his head. "Very strong. Six hundred people at once? Very, very strong."

Erin flashed a brilliant smile. "Hey, I conquered the seas for a decade with only two people. You got a lot more than that, plus your swordwork, Riley...This magician doesn't know the trouble he's in."

"I gotta agree with the lady." William put his hand on

Riley's shoulder. "Plus, we got me. Rendal doesn't stand a fuckin' chance with all that on our side."

Riley rolled her eyes and looked at Twocuts. "What are you planning on doing?"

"I was plannin' on leavin'. Whatever that man is doin', I don't want no part of it. What are *you* plannin' on doin'?"

"I'm planning on kicking this mage's ass, that's what."

CHAPTER SEVEN

Mason stood behind Rendal. He hated the man and wanted to just tip him over the rail right fucking now, but he knew it would be futile. The mage would levitate or some other bullshit and end up hurting Mason.

So, he stood in the bow behind the evil mage and listened for the man to pontificate.

"It's nice, isn't it?" Rendal asked.

"Do you ever bore yourself?" Mason quipped.

"Of course not. I find my conversation riveting."

Must be easy since you're the only person who ever talks, Mason thought but did not say aloud.

"I mean, look around you. Do you see my power?"

Mason didn't want to look. The wind was whipping past his face as the ship plunged across the water, and he only wanted to stare straight ahead. To look to either side might prove the man right.

Insane or not, Mason understood his power.

"What other person on the planet could do this?"

Mason said nothing.

He watched as Rendal looked to his left.

"Don't you want to see?" Rendal pointed his finger to the left and Mason felt his head turning. He couldn't stop it.

Two ships sat in the water—large ones, full of people.

"Watch them wave," Rendal quipped.

Because it was all bullshit.

Mason saw the men on deck wave at Rendal's ship. The necklaces they all wore lit bright enough for him to see, because Rendal was in control of their every move.

"Right now I'm in their heads." The mage put his hand down, and Mason regained mastery over his neck. Rendal kept talking. "Has Harold told you where we're heading yet?"

Mason knew the man could read his thoughts. There wasn't any need to speak to him; everything Rendal did was for control. To instill fear in Mason.

"You may not bore yourself, Rendal, but you bore me. I don't give a fuck where we're going, because Riley is on the way. I don't know how many times I have to tell you that or why you make me keep repeating myself."

Rendal spoke as if he hadn't heard the Assistant Prefect. "And what I find spectacular is it's not taking *that* much energy."

Mason thought he knew why. He'd seen Rendal wearing a green bracelet and a red one, but now he had two green bracelets pushed close together on his wrist.

They were brightly lit, as was the red one was on his other arm.

Mason didn't know how all this worked, but he thought the green ones were giving him extra power somehow while the red one connected him to the other ships.

"You're powerful because you have those bracelets, but if you tossed them over the side, you wouldn't be able to do any of this." Mason sneered. "You don't hold the power, those pieces of jewelry do."

Rendal turned around, smiling. "When Riley uses her sword to protect your pimply ass, do you say *she* has no power? Or do you simply thank her? I'm enhancing my gifts, true, but so does Riley with her sword."

Rendal stepped a bit closer.

"You know that when she joins me, she's going to get bracelets like these, right? Even if she came at me with magic right now, I'm too powerful. The things I can do dwarf her natural abilities, and when she sees that, she'll join."

Mason laughed. "You forget what happened at your compound, don't you?"

Rendal's eyes narrowed, but he remained quiet.

"We were all about to die. Even then your power was too great for us, for Worth or William or even Riley. And what did she do, Rendal the all-powerful mage? She fought back. She charged you as if you were nothing more than a regular soldier. She threw a fucking axe into your arm."

Mason stepped closer as well, putting his face right in front of the mage's, though he knew it was dangerous.

"I know Riley, and I know you now. The two of you are nothing alike. You hid like a coward in the wilderness for years, building an army that you thought would be unstoppable. You know the difference between you and her? She'll come for you by herself with a damn steak knife if it means she has a chance of killing you. She doesn't need bracelets or magic. The difference, grand mage, is that she's a warrior, and you're just a child trying to get back at Daddy for punishing you when you stepped out of line."

Rendal didn't move, but his eyes blazed red.

Mason rose thirty feet above the deck, and his throat tightened as if a hand had grabbed it and cut the oxygen flow off.

Watch yourself, boy, Rendal's voice spat inside his head. *Be careful with that wagging tongue, or you might find it ripped right out of your throat.*

Mason felt his tongue being pulled out of his mouth as if held by a pair of pliers.

You toy with others, but not me. You rule others, but not me. You're here to bring Riley to me, but other than that, you have no value.

Mason's tongue withdrew into his mouth and the grip on his throat was reduced, but his body moved over the ship so that he hung above blue water.

There's no help out here. Only pirates, me, and the sharks. I'll give you to them and find another way to get Riley if you keep yipping. Understand?

Mason made no movement, just remembered Riley's strength and thought three words: *Go fuck yourself.*

His body floated back down to the deck. His throat was slightly swollen.

Harold was standing behind him now as if he'd appeared from thin air.

"Hello, Harold." Rendal's voice was calm, the spite gone. "Please take Mason belowdecks. *Way* below. Put him in a cage all by himself. He needs to learn some manners."

"Of course, sir," Harold replied.

Harold grabbed Mason's arm, but he pulled back, not letting himself be dragged away so easily.

"Rendal, you still don't scare me. Feed me to the sharks or let me live, it makes no difference. You're in Riley's sights now, and that means it's over for you, whether you realize it or not."

Rendal turned around, his voice soft as if nothing Mason said mattered in the slightest. "Everybody talks. Only action matters, my dear Assistant Prefect."

Harold threw Mason in with the rest of the prisoners. They were on the lowest of the ship's three levels, and cages lined the sides. People from the compound sat in the cages wearing their green necklaces. Rendal's workers came and went from these levels, feeding, cleaning, and taking prisoners to be drained.

Harold thought this Mason fellow was very close to finding himself on the bad side of his master, and that meant he might be drained soon too. He'd lose the nanocytes his blood carried. Harold didn't know if those things replicated or if once gone…

Poof! No more magic potential.

"I do not care whether you live or die," Harold stated as he tossed the man into the cage. "But if I can give you any advice, I'd watch your mouth around him. He's treating you kindly, and you'd be wise to remember that. It could get worse for you."

The man looked at his feet and smiled. "You're the one who came for Riley?"

"I did." Harold nodded.

"Then you know, perhaps better than anyone else, it's going to get a lot worse for all of you on this ship." Mason looked up, his eyes fierce. "She's coming, Harold buddy, and she's not going to look kindly on you either."

Harold only stared at the man for another second, then turned and left the prison level.

He didn't want to think about the Assistant Prefect's words. Didn't want them in his mind.

Harold had made his decision, and the man downstairs was delusional if he thought Riley could challenge Rendal. Perhaps once, before all his technology came to be.

Now, though?

Impossible.

Harold had never imagined anyone could be this strong. Letting Mason's thoughts into his own would be horrendous. Rendal would know, if he didn't already.

He climbed back up the ladders to the upper deck. He knew Rendal still wanted to see him.

"I've put him with the others, sir. What else can I do?"

"We're going to reach that cove by tomorrow night, I think, if everything goes as it should." Rendal's back was to Harold; he was seemingly content to simply stare out at the water. "She's there."

"The Right Hand?" Harold asked.

"No, the whore you fucked last time you were in Sidnie. *Yes,* the Right Hand, Harold. Are you losing your wits, man?"

"My apologies, sir. I just wanted to make sure."

Rendal smiled. "I'm just giving you a hard time. But, yes, Riley is there. She's got her crew, plus more. Many mages."

"It doesn't matter what she has, sir."

Rendal chuckled. "That's the spirit. But she is going to try to make a stand, I fear. She will try to break through our offense and steal back her precious Mason."

Harold knew that the mage wasn't telling him everything. He was holding some of the plan back, ensuring that only he knew everything when the time came.

"What do you want me to do?"

"Make a path for her," Rendal answered. "But only her. I don't want the rest of her crew getting on the ship, you understand?"

"Yes, sir. I understand."

"Good. I don't care how many of us die to ensure she comes alone, but make sure she does. We have more than enough to replenish any losses, and we'll continue gathering soldiers."

Harold nodded. "I'll make sure it happens."

The damn problem was *how* to make sure it happened.

Harold didn't have a clue. He had one day to figure it out and had no idea of the land's layout, nor how to lure the Right Hand away from her crew.

"This is a pickle, boss." Belarus stared at the map in front of him. He and Harold were both looking at it, the paper showing the island they'd arrive at tomorrow.

"A pickle is what's between your legs, Belarus," Harold mocked. "This is what adults call 'a problem.'"

"Aye, that's what I mean, boss. A real problem."

Harold wondered how he was supposed to work with an idiot beneath him.

"The master says that there will be ships here, here, and here. Also along these edges." Harold marked the paper with a piece of chalk. "He says that Riley and her crew will hole up here, in the middle."

He circled a building in the center.

"Why are they holin' up there? Why ain't they fleein'? Makes no sense, ya ask me, boss."

Harold closed his eyes, doing his best to keep from bashing the moron's brains in. "No one is asking you, Belarus. No one will *ever* ask you your opinion, not in this room and not on this ship. You are to follow orders; is that clear?"

"'Course, boss. Just thinkin' aloud."

"Well, stop." Harold was growing angrier by the second, and the fact that Belarus didn't care only intensified it. "Now listen…we're going to have casualties. A lot of them, and the master is fine with that. But she *is* to make it up this trail here, and by the end, she is to be by herself. You understand?"

Belarus insisted that he did, indeed, get it.

Now Harold just needed to make sure *he* wasn't one of the people dying when that bitch ripped her way north to the ship.

CHAPTER EIGHT

"This big dumb animal is going to get us all killed." Lucie was staring at William, not an ounce of friendliness on her face.

"I'm sorry, Lucie," William retorted. "Down there at your restaurant, did you learn military tactics along with how to make stew?"

Lucie's eyes grew red, and Riley stepped between the two.

"Hey, both of you, *quit* it. We're not going to kill ourselves before the mage gets here, you understand?"

William turned from Lucie to Riley. "What she's sayin' is crazy, Riley, and you know it. None of our training, none of our *experience*, says we hole up here while Rendal's army swarms the island. He'll take every ship and every man but us, then simply sail off into the sunset, heading right for New Perth with Mason in tow."

Lucie's eyes returned to their normal color and she looked at Riley, who was the de facto leader now.

"That makes sense in a normal battle. This *isn't* a

normal battle. Rendal is gathering men, that's true, but that ain't all he's doin', girl. He's after *you* above all else. He wants *you*. That's why the oaf here is wrong."

"He might be an oaf, Lucie, but he's our oaf, so cool it," Riley responded.

"Aye, I'll show you both an oaf if you don't watch your mouths." William grinned despite his challenge. They were on the same side, and William wasn't too stubborn to forget that.

"Okay. You're right." Lucie's voice calmed. "But that doesn't change the facts. Rendal wants you. He's not leaving this place without you, because he knows you're here. His power is growing, and I can't cast a mental block strong enough to keep him fully out. He wants troops, but he wants you more."

"And if we stay in here?" Riley asked.

They currently were in the middle of the island, inhabiting the largest building (though small by New Perth standards). It was a circular dome, unused for the most part.

Erin said it was used for pirate matters, a neutral meeting place when things grew too heated.

Verith and his troops were guarding the outer perimeter while Riley's group talked inside.

"If we stay here," Lucie answered, "*he* will have to come get you or send others to do so. *Here* we can defend ourselves. Out there, have you seen much of the island?"

Riley looked at Erin. "What's it like?"

"The places that are inhabited are like what you've seen, but beyond that, it's basically jungle," Erin answered.

"Exactly," Lucie kept going. "From what Twocuts tells

us, he'll be here tomorrow night, which means that if one of us gets lost in that jungle, we might be lost for good."

"Speak for yourselves," William said with a grin. "Got my sword and my fire, and I ain't scared of burnin' down no trees."

Lucie rolled her eyes and kept going. "If we stay in here and guard this as our base, he won't leave. He'll have to come."

Erin spoke up. "I don't know anything about this mage, just what you've all said, and Twocuts. But if we're in here and he comes, how are we going to defend ourselves?"

"My lady," William said. "We'll do what Right Hands do. We'll kill whoever he sends."

Riley looked away quickly, her hand moving to her mouth to hide the smile.

My lady, she thought. *He's head over heels for this woman.*

Riley got control of herself and turned back to the group.

"My lady," she said. She was unable to help herself, and the grin reappeared. "We have Worth and his magicians. We have Twocuts and an entire pirate army. We can hold them off until Rendal gets here."

"And then what?" Erin asked.

"I'm going to twist his balls until either I rip them off or he gives me Mason." Riley grinned, and Erin's beautiful smile flashed over her face.

"That sounds just about right."

The night grew late, and Riley was alone. She'd walked

outside, her sword on her hip. She wasn't worried about the island now.

Twocuts had sent word of what was coming, and that anyone who didn't want to fight this new tyrant should leave. If you did want to fight and you stayed, all pirates were one team until this threat was removed.

So for perhaps the first time in its history, the island wasn't full of danger.

Riley hadn't tried training with Worth in days. William had. He'd been doing it every night, and his skills were definitely improving.

Eric had taken part tonight, and Worth was teaching him how to bring his fire to life when he wasn't in battle.

Everyone's magic was growing except hers.

She—the person that Rendal wanted so badly— apparently couldn't light a single flame unless William was about to die.

Riley pulled her sword from her hip and surveyed the green stones in the hilt, still not understanding exactly how they could help her.

Yet, the sword was better than her last. She held no doubt about that.

With her old sword, she probably would have lost to Eric out there. With this one she'd been able to do more, but she didn't understand *how*.

It magic. Or will be. When you magic.

Worth had told her that, but the proclaimed greatest mage on the continent could do nothing without death rearing its head.

"You worry."

Riley spun, her sword flipping up and out.

She caught it just before it sliced off Worth's head.

He smiled at her through purple lips. He still held his wine chalice, not a drop spilled. "You worry. Too much."

"Worth, what the *hell*, man? I almost cut your head off."

"Worth no worry. That why Worth happy." He took a light sip from his chalice. "Why you worry for tomorrow?"

"I can't tell if you're playing dumb or you really don't know." Riley sheathed her sword, the metal barely making any noise against the leather.

"Maybe both. Maybe neither. Why you worry?" Worth asked again.

"Because *he's* coming, and I know what he did last time. I gave everything I had. Hell, we *all* gave everything we had, but it wasn't enough. He stole the person I care for most in the world."

"Mason, aye?" Worth questioned.

"Yes, Mason."

Worth smiled wide. "You worry. Too much. You, Mason, marry. Make babies."

Riley felt heat rising from her chest to her cheeks and could only hope the night sky hid it from Worth.

"It's not like that, Worth."

"Never is in beginning. That why it works. You really love him." Worth's smile was wide, and he was speaking loudly as if this was well known.

Riley didn't need to turn around to understand they were alone. Her senses told her well enough.

Still, Worth was talking crazy.

"Come. Walk with Worth."

The bald man went to his right, lifting his chalice to his lips and not bothering to look at Riley.

She waited for a second, then caught up with the tent man.

They walked in silence for some time, until they reached the edge of the jungle. Worth didn't stop but kept going forward.

His eyes lit red, and the vines and tree limbs moved out of his way. Riley stuck close behind, ensuring that she passed through the same small path.

Worth led the two of them deep into the jungle, but finally they found a small clearing—a circle about twelve feet wide. No tree branches stretched across above them, revealing the open sky.

"How did you know this was here?" she asked.

Worth shrugged. "Didn't. Just went for walk."

Riley's eyes narrowed. She didn't know if she believed him. She also didn't know how this clearing existed, even the tree branches above not entering the circle.

Worth sat down, folding his legs beneath him.

"How can you be so fat but move so easily?" Riley smiled as she followed suit.

Worth laughed. "Magic."

"Why are we out here, Worth?" Riley asked.

"You bad student." He nodded, but the grimness from days earlier was missing. "Stubborn. Don't listen to Worth."

"I try," Riley answered. "I really do. I don't know why I can't do magic."

"Worth know. Worth smart. You…" He shook his head and looked at the ground. "Not so smart."

He was grinning.

"At least I'm not fat."

Worth nodded. "Fat and stupid be bad. I fat. You stupid.

Good plan."

Riley laughed, her mind losing its earlier doubts.

"He come tomorrow." Worth's smile disappeared, and he looked into his wine chalice. "He want you. Lucie speak true. You don't need worry. Worry too much, Worth thinks."

"I can't beat him with my sword. Not even the one you gave me," Riley explained. "I can help. I can support you and your mages, but one on one? I don't know what I can do."

"Each time you stop him, aye?" Worth asked.

"It depends on what you mean by stop."

"He kill you?"

Riley shook her head.

"No. He no kill you. He kill Mason? He kill William? He kill Lucie?"

Riley shook her head again.

"No," Worth continued. "You magic, Riley. You no see it, but it true. Those you care about, they no die, even when powerful mage attack. They live. You live. *Worth* live. You see that magic?"

Riley chuckled. "That's not magic, Worth. That's luck. Stupid luck."

"No. Stupid Riley." Worth grinned. "*That* magic. You change battlefield by showing up. Nothing else. *You* magic."

"But not like you. Not like William. Not like Lucie."

"Not *yet*, but we not change battlefield. We piece of battlefield. You beyond it." Worth extended his chalice to Riley. "Drink."

Riley had never seen him offer a drink to anyone.

Riley grinned. "Did you take me out here to try and get

fresh, Worth?"

"No. You no Worth type. Too skinny. Now drink."

Riley laughed and took the chalice from the strange mage. She looked down and saw the purple liquid.

She nodded at Worth. "Thank you."

Riley took a deep drink. The wine was good, but one swig was enough. She tried to pull away, but Worth's hand forced the chalice up.

"More."

Riley listened, his hand helping to guide the rest of the liquid down.

Finally, when all the wine was gone, Worth let her lower the chalice.

Riley's head was already buzzing. She hardly *ever* drank. The alcohol had hit her immediately.

"Now. No more worry tonight. You bad student, but even bad student need rest."

Worth smiled, and Riley smiled right back.

"You see them?"

Riley nodded. She held the telescope to her eye.

The sun was falling but wasn't quite gone.

Four ships had just crossed the horizon. Each had a different flag flying high, but only one mattered: the green circular ring over a black background.

Rendal's ship.

"Quit hoggin' it, skinny." William stood next to Riley.

She handed over the telescope.

William put it to his eye. "Aye, there they are. Rendal

has some balls on 'im, that's for sure."

"Why do you say that?" Verith asked.

William took the telescope from his face, grinning. "Because he's goin' up against me. I bet he's literally pissin' his pants right now. Has a team of people followin' him around to clean it all up."

Riley laughed.

"Aye, landlubbers."

She turned around and saw Twocuts walking across the deck. They were on his ship again; it was the largest docked at the island, and the one with the clearest view of Rendal's oncoming armada.

"Captain," Riley responded.

"Ya see 'em out there on the horizon?" Twocuts asked.

"We see them." Riley stepped forward and shook the pirate's offered hand. It wasn't a move she thought she'd ever make, but the man had a certain honor.

The *ocean* held a different code, one that 'landlubbers' didn't recognize but most pirates adhered to. Right now their way of life was being threatened, so regardless of the flag that flew over their ship, the pirates were pitching in.

"We're about to move muh ship," Twocuts commented as he walked to the rail. "This thing is far too precious to be at the front when he arrives."

"Where ya puttin' it?" William grumbled. "Thinkin' about just sailin' off?"

Twocuts chuckled. "Ye landlubbers got less trust than pirates. I'm movin' the ship to the opposite side of the island. We'll dock before he gets here."

"Ya know the plan?" William asked gruffly.

"Aye, William, Right Hand of Such and Such, I know the

plan."

"You don't seem nervous." William stepped forward, his aggression coming out. He really didn't trust these pirates.

The captain turned around, his smile gone.

"You see my throat, doncha? I don't put makeup on each morning to make it look like this. No, each mornin' I wake up, and I'm reminded that I should be twice dead already. But I'm not—I'm alive. This magician or mage or whatever ya wanna call him may be strong, but he ain't no match for Twocuts or the banner I fly."

"William, he sounds exactly like you." Riley spoke up, grinning. "You two should be friends."

"Sounds like me, but don't look like me. I'm more handsome." William turned around, apparently satisfied with the pirate's answers. "We got our own stuff to worry 'bout now. Verith, walk me through the plan."

Riley, Verith, and William started toward the gangplank so Twocuts could prepare to move the ship.

"The core group is going to remain in the island's center." Verith walked behind Riley and William. "You two, Worth, Lucie, and Erin. I'm taking Eric with me."

"Why?" Riley asked. She didn't like the idea of the young pirate leaving, although she didn't quite know why. Perhaps because he was so young, or perhaps because he'd only known death his whole life?

"You got a thing for the lad?" William grinned from ear to ear.

"Zip it, William. Why is he going out there with you, Verith?" Riley was serious. She wanted to know.

"We need every able-bodied man we can get, Riley," Verith answered. "Eric is young, but he's dangerous.

Extremely so. His swordwork alone puts him in the top ten percent of my men, and with his magic abilities, he might be the best. We need him on the frontlines."

"Have you talked to Erin?"

Verith nodded. "She agrees. She wants him to help."

"Hey, Riley. Think about it. You could marry him, and I could marry Erin at the same ceremony." William was barely holding in his laughter.

"It's going to be hard to find anyone to marry you after I cut your dick off." Riley let her anger go. She wasn't in love with Eric, just protective. Still, Verith was right. He was an excellent fighter, and they would need to hold off Rendal's assault for as long as possible.

Until Rendal arrived at the island's center.

"Finish the plan, Verith. Maybe this woman will quit interruptin' ya for a second," William said.

The group stepped off the ship as Verith continued, "The mages are going to work to create a mental shield over much of the island. Now, I don't know how that all works—not really, but Worth says they can do it. It'll keep Rendal from possessing all of us immediately or whatever the hell he's doing. We're anticipating that he'll send foot soldiers in, and we're going to attack them."

"'We're?' Just us?" William asked.

"No. The pirates are throwing in too. Four captains are agreeing to help, but there's no one leader. Basically, they refuse to follow anyone else, which will work out. We're using a four-pronged approach to the northern half of the island, trying to kill as many as we can before Rendal actually exits the ship."

Verith grew quiet for a second, then looked at Riley.

"All of this is assuming Lucie is right. We're assuming that Rendal is coming to get you. There are a few options that could happen. We could beat them back and actually go aboard *his* ship ourselves. If that happens, it will probably all end. I imagine that we have the men to do it. We'll outnumber him.

"The other possibility is that we can't hold them and they slowly beat *us* back. We'll take heavy casualties, and eventually break completely. It's important to remember that one side is going to break, and if they're stronger, getting Rendal out of that ship quickly is what we want."

"And if he doesn't come out?" Riley asked.

"Then we'll all die, and he'll sail off into the sunset with a larger army," Verith answered.

"So you're sayin' that Lucie better fuckin' be right?" William grumbled.

"That's what I'm saying."

"Aye," William muttered. "Hate to admit it, but I think the old woman prolly is. That Rendal has a hankerin' for ya, Riley. He'll come. Verith and his crew just need to hold his troops until he does."

"I just wanted to tell you the possibilities." Verith's eyes, hard like steel, were focused ahead. "We'll hold them. We'll make sure he gets to you."

<hr>

Runners came and went.

Riley and her core group remained at the island's center, but runners brought them information from the outside.

Verith sent the largest number, men coming and going almost constantly, but the pirates sent emissaries too.

Riley remained seated, her eyes closed much of the time.

She didn't open them when the runners entered the room. She was no general. She was a Right Hand and hadn't been extensively trained in strategy.

"You're sure?"

She heard William's gruff voice from the other side of the room.

"Aye, I'm sure, landlubber," the pirate runner answered. He was out of breath, and Riley opened her eyes to look at him.

He had a large gash on his right arm; something had ripped through both his leather guard and his flesh. He was bleeding and his skin pale, but he didn't appear to be near fainting.

"What is it?" she asked.

"They're breaking through." William didn't turn around. "Fucking Rendal's people are breaking through."

"I'm going up top." Riley stood from her chair.

"It's too dangerous." William whipped around to face her.

Atop the building was a pirate's lookout, just like the kind they used on their ships. Whether it was decor or actually of use, Riley didn't know. Either way, she would be able to see the entire island from that vantage point.

"You've got to be kidding me." She raised an eyebrow at William. "We're Right Hands, man. Not princesses."

William smiled. "Father and Mother, what is happening to me? I been listenin' to Lucie for too long."

"Ya ain't been listenin' to me *enough*," Lucie called from the other side of the room. She hadn't interfered with anything, although her eyes had been blazing red the entire time. They still were, and Riley knew why—she was supporting the other mages in keeping up a mental shield against Rendal. "It is too dangerous for her up there. She needs to be inside, especially if they're breaking through now. It means Rendal will come soon."

Riley looked at her. "I'm sorry, Lucie, but I can't just sit in here anymore. If Rendal is breaking through, people are dying, at least partially because *I'm* in *here.* I'm going upstairs to see for myself what is happening."

Lucie only stared at her with those red eyes, saying nothing.

"About time you grew a pair. Let's go." William headed toward the circular stairs in the middle of the room. They wrapped around a pole that led up.

"If I *had* a pair, chubby, you know they'd be bigger than yours." She looked at Erin and Worth, neither of whom had said anything. "Either of you want to come?"

Erin shook her head. "Someone has to be here for the runners."

Worth's eyes were red, and sweat lay on his brow. "He strong. Grow stronger, too. Worth stay."

William started to climb, and Riley followed. Up and up they went, twisting around the pole. Riley saw fire blazing across the island, trees burning brightly against the night sky. A cannonball streaked through the air; whether it was Rendal's ship or her allies', who could tell?

It took a few minutes but they reached the lookout perch, a round cup-like structure.

Riley's breath caught in her throat.

"No…"

"Maybe it looks worse than it is?" Even William was finding it hard to keep any optimism in his voice.

Riley's sharp eyes showed her everything she needed to see. She saw Rendal's ship at the north end of the island, and burnt buildings, trees, and every other obstacle from the docks onward.

She could see his troops—if they could be called that. Red necklaces adorned them all, and their eyes were as red as Lucie's. Fire and electricity ripped from their hands, even their eyes.

Worth's mages had spread out and were fighting back, but there were so *few* of them.

The pirates' and Verith's men were harder to see, yet she heard the clangs of their steel.

"We have to do something." Riley's face grew calm, everything except her eyes. They raged. "Lucie is wrong. We can't sit here and let these people be slaughtered, even if Rendal does come for me."

"At last, she sees the fuckin' light! I been tellin' you that the whole time! You need to just start listenin' to me and ignorin' the rest of these fools." William had turned from the carnage below and was grinning at Riley. "We can get 'em right now. We'll cut through his troops like a knife through butter."

Riley looked at the war raging in front of her.

Rendal wanted her.

That was true.

And he had Mason.

Sitting here any longer was idiotic.

If Rendal wanted her, then she'd go to him.

"Let's fuck this guy up." Riley's face was furious as she walked back down the staircase.

When they reached the bottom, Riley's mind was already in warrior mode. She saw the people in the room as objects, not caring what they did as long as they stayed out of her way.

Mason was to the north, and she'd just sat in here waiting for the mage to come to her.

Nonsense.

All of it had been nonsense.

"Don't go." Lucie's eyes still held magic, but her face held concern.

Riley said nothing, just went to the wall where weapons hung. She grabbed a long knife and shoved it through her belt. There was a pair of handcuffs, too; she assumed they were used when a pirate needed to be subdued. She looped them around her belt as well.

"We're goin', Lucie." William grabbed a shield from the wall, testing its weight in his left hand. He looked at Riley and grinned. "Want to try somethin' with this."

"Just kill his people, and we should be all right."

"That ain't gonna be a problem, skinny. I'll easily send twice as many to the Mother and Father as you. Don't worry about *that* at all."

"Riley, *please*," Lucie pleaded. "You going to him—it's what he wants."

Riley turned from the wall and stared at the old woman.

"He wants *you*," Lucie continued. "All this is about *you*. About your magic. You want to face him on *your* playing field, not his. If you go to him, you'll be on *his*. That's what he wants you to do. It's why he's still on that damned ship. He's waiting for you."

"Then I won't keep him waiting any longer. You know I won't stand here and let others die for me. I came on this voyage to get Mason back, and that's exactly what I plan to do. I love you, and more, I respect you…but I'm going out there." Riley's voice was as cold as the steel at her side.

Lucie stared for a second longer. She saw the determination and knew the Right Hand would not be persuaded to do anything else. "Good luck, Riley. It was an honor."

"Oh, hush, you old biddy." William pulled the broadsword from his back. "We're going to go get your old lover, cut his nuts off, and put 'em in a jar for you. You can hold onto 'em for the rest of your life if you like. Hell, put 'em on the bar at your restaurant and let the rest of the world see 'em." He looked at Riley. "She worries too much. Let's go."

The two Right Hands left the safety of their building and went out into the world to do battle.

"She's coming, sir." Harold stood in front of Rendal. He'd been *terrified* for the past couple of hours. He and Belarus had created a plan to lead the woman directly to them, but then the bitch hadn't left the damned building. She'd simply *remained* there.

It was going to be hard to get her on *this* ship if she didn't leave *that* building.

Literally, Harold had been sweating. To come back to

Rendal and tell him the bitch wasn't exiting and that Harold didn't know what to do?

Well, Harold might as well go ahead and try to join one of the pirate ships around here, because he would be as good as dead to Rendal.

And then a runner had given him word.

She's out of the building and moving north.

You're sure it's her? Harold had asked.

Yeah. She's with the big man. He's got fire on his sword and shield.

That was all Harold needed to hear; he went to Rendal.

"I knew you wouldn't fail me, Harold." The mage sat alone in his chambers. His eyes were closed when Harold entered, but he opened then now. Red blazed across them. "The mages are making it hard for me to see her. Do you know how long before she gets to us?"

"Thirty minutes." Harold was sure about that. "We're giving ground across her path, and she's...well, *deadly*, sir."

"Ah, yes, she is. I'll see her in thirty minutes, Harold. You did good work."

"Thank you, sir."

***

"Duck!"

Riley heard William's yell and reacted; she dropped to a knee as fire flashed over her head. She turned around and saw a man standing with a hand-axe stuck in his head, fire blazing across it.

"That's number one!" William called.

"One what?" Riley asked, standing.

"One time I've saved your life, skinny. I'm keepin' track, and when this is over, everyone's gonna know about it!"

He turned, catching an attacker with his shield. Fire burned brightly across the metal, and the attacker was soon in flames and shrieking.

"You ready? Tired of waitin' for you." William was grinning. Sweat dripped from his forehead, but he showed no signs of tiring.

Riley quickly scanned the area around them. They'd been heading north, but veered slightly east and ran into a group of Rendal's people. They all lay dead around the Right Hands' feet now.

"Try to keep up, chubby," she told William and took off. She moved through the night like the wind, silent and unseen.

They came across another small group of soldiers and, Riley leading, dispatched them easily. Most of them didn't even have time to scream.

"Save some for me!" William called from ten feet behind her.

"Run faster!"

She was grinning, having fun killing the wicked. They were making progress, and the path wasn't that hard. War raged around her, but in this part of the jungle, they moved quickly.

Heading directly to Rendal's ship.

Minutes passed, and the fire on William's weapon and shield died. They moved quietly, quickly, a virus heading directly to the heart of the beast.

They left the jungle at the docks.

The ship floated in front of them, and a flag flew high above—a green ring on a black background.

The docks were empty, and despite the background noise of war, Riley heard nothing but the wind and sloshing water.

"Where is everyone?" William asked.

"Fighting," Riley answered.

"Onward, then." William's face was grim with determination.

Riley grabbed his arm. "Hold on. This makes no sense."

"The hell you talkin' 'bout? 'Course it makes sense. He sent his armies out there, and that's why no one is here." William tried to move forward, but Riley's iron grip held him in place.

"Look!" she whispered harshly. "Look at that ship. What do you see?"

William was quiet as they stared at it.

The answer was obvious, now that they weren't gung-ho about going aboard and murdering everyone until they found Mason.

A single light was on inside. A *single* one.

The rest of the ship was dark.

The light was near the ship's bow, a porthole showing candles burning inside.

"He's in there." William pointed with his sword. "That's him."

Riley knew it was true. "But why? Why is he alone?"

"Does it fuckin' matter? If he's alone, we go kill him. That's why we came up here, ain't it?" William was growing angry, not wanting to remain standing at the docks any longer.

"Look at the door. It's wide open, William. It's *asking* for people to come in." Riley didn't like this at all. The run here had been far too easy. They'd been attacked once—but only when they veered slightly off course. As long as they headed directly north, there'd been almost no problems. "Lucie was right. This is a trap."

William whipped around, his full height and weight apparent as he looked down at Riley.

"I don't give a fuck if it's a trap," he growled. "I don't give a fuck if Rendal has five hundred flying fairies in there, each of them shooting electricity out of their ass and having bloodlust on their mind. The Assistant Prefect is in there, so we're goin' in. Trap, no trap, Lucie, no Lucie— we're goin' in."

"I *know* Mason is in there. You don't have to tell me. What I'm saying is, are we going to save him by marching in or are we going to get ourselves killed?" Riley didn't fear walking onto that ship.

She feared walking into a trap and not saving the man she'd pledged her life to.

"I'm goin' in. You can come or stay here." With that, William started toward the docks.

Riley didn't hesitate. She went forward as well.

Something loud crashed behind her, but she didn't turn to look. Everything that mattered was in front of her, so her focus had to be there.

They went aboard the ship, then climbed down a ladder inside and stopped. It was darker there, and they let their eyes adjust.

"The only danger on this thing is trippin' and breakin' an ankle. I don't know why you're so scared, skinny. Ain't no one even here." William grinned, and the two started moving again.

Riley listened with both her mind and ears. She wondered if Rendal would reach out to her as he had before, filling her head with his voice.

All she heard were the ship's creaks and their footsteps as they moved toward the hatch the light emerged from.

"Hey." William was walking in front. "I ain't mean nothin' bout Mason being on here. I know you're dedicated. I just also knew it would getcha on the ship, and I'm lookin' to kick some ass."

"Yeah, yeah. You got me on. The problem is, I'm not sure you can kick much ass," Riley shot back.

"Don't make me turn around, Riley. I'll bend you over my knee like you're my daughter."

"More like granddaughter, old man. Surprised your knees were able to get you through that jungle. Thought they were gonna break, from the way they were poppin'.'"

The two let the joking subside and went down the ladder silently, then kept going forward, Riley sure they were on the right level.

Riley saw the door. Light shone from inside, flooding out through its sides.

Both Right Hands stopped.

"You ready?" William asked.

"Born ready, chubby. Let's go kill the sonofabitch."

"I'll go first. I've got the shield," William whispered.

"And the bigger belly." Riley smiled. "You'll be able to block anything he throws with multiple defenses."

William grinned. "When I'm done with him, you and I are gonna tango."

"Go on, big man. Let's finish this."

William looked down at his feet, gathering himself. He took a deep breath and then started forward, gaining speed as he went.

His footsteps pounded on the floor and Riley followed right behind, her sword ready and her mind focused like a hawk searching for prey.

William brought his shield up and hit the door full force. It burst open, splinters flying everywhere. He brought his sword down in a deadly arc to kill whoever stood in front of him, sight unseen.

Riley spilled to the right.

And then they stopped.

The mage was in front of them.

He sat in a chair, his arms resting lazily at his sides. His eyes were closed despite the door's explosion. He hadn't moved an inch.

"Where is Mason?" Riley said, stepping past William.

Rendal opened his eyes. "Hello, Riley."

"Fuck this," William growled. He lifted his sword to swing, ready to take the mage's head off.

"No." Riley's voice slashed through the room. "Not until we know where Mason is."

William stayed his sword.

"Tell me." Riley's own sword was loose in her hand. The mage's eyes were red, but she felt no fear—only determination.

"He's downstairs with the rest."

"Take us to him. Now." Riley stood about five feet from the mage.

"I'd rather talk to you for a minute." Rendal smiled.

"How about we do that?"

"If he's downstairs, we'll find him. Let's kill this bastard." Fire rolled from William's hands to his sword.

Rendal's red eyes didn't move from Riley as he spoke. "Hush, child."

Riley heard William's sword and shield hit the ground. She simultaneously stepped back from the mage and looked at William, not understanding.

William's hands were at his throat, and his mouth was wide open.

Riley's gaze flashed to Rendal. She didn't think, only moved. She crossed the room in rapid steps and put her sword to the mage's throat. "Whatever the fuck you're doing to him, stop."

Rendal didn't move, only grinned. "Of course, Right Hand."

Riley heard William drop. She turned her head, not moving the sword from Rendal's neck.

William lay on the floor, his eyes closed. She saw his chest moving, so he was still breathing.

"He's asleep. It's quite okay. No harm has come to your partner."

Riley looked at the mage, who made no movement. "Mason. Where is he?"

"Do you see what I'm doing yet, Riley?" the mage asked, completely ignoring her question.

"I don't give a fuck what you're doing. I want to know where Mason is, and then I'm hauling you to New Perth for trial. *Where is he?*"

"Everything you love is going to fall apart." Rendal nodded, still grinning. "I want you to understand that right now. I want it to be crystal clear. I'm going to take and take and take from you until there is nothing left. I'm going to steal it all, and you're going to watch…or you're going to join me."

"Never. I'll never join you, Rendal. I'm considering forsaking the trial and simply executing you right now."

Rendal chuckled. "So strong, yet so naive. You're here because I want you to be. You're in this room holding this sword because I wanted it to happen. You will no more execute me than your friend over there would."

She pressed the sword's blade deeper into his throat, and Rendal kept smiling.

"Take my hand, and this can stop. Bow before me, and I'll give you Mason back. I'll even give you New Perth if you want it. You can rule it however you prefer, Riley. It'll be yours; all you have to do is take a knee and kiss my hand."

"You can kiss my ass, Rendal. Where is the Assistant Prefect?"

Rendal nodded. "You're having trouble with magic, aren't you? You're unable to use it properly. Only when under horrible stress, otherwise, it's dormant. Am I right?"

Blood dripped from Rendal's neck.

Riley hadn't realized she'd pressed harder at his question.

The mage only smiled.

"I can show you how to use it, Riley. I can show you better than that bald man or Lucie. I can give you the power you've never understood."

"You can give me nothing." She spat on him as she spoke. "You're nothing like me. You're no mentor. You're no fucking father figure. You're evil, and I'm going to end you so you never harm anyone else."

Riley took a deep breath and then pulled back, releasing him. There was a red line on Rendal's neck, but he paid it no mind.

Riley reached to the back of her belt and removed the cuffs she'd taken off the wall.

"Rendal Hemmons, you're under arrest for kidnapping Assistant Prefect Mason Ire, conspiracy against New Perth, and...Well, and a whole bunch of other fucking crimes I'm not going to list. Stand up, turn around, and put your hands behind your back."

Rendal sighed. "You still don't understand, but okay. I will show you."

He stood up slowly and did as she commanded. The mage placed his hands behind his back.

Riley stepped forward. She glanced at William; he was still breathing, apparently asleep.

She grabbed Rendal's left hand hard and brought the cuffs down.

Riley felt it a moment before it happened—nanoseconds. She saw the green bracelet light up on Rendal's right wrist, and then *everything* in the room rose into the air.

She flew backward, rising and then floating in the middle of the room. Riley couldn't move. Couldn't swing her sword, couldn't even open her mouth.

Everything else floated too. The chair Rendal had sat on. Lanterns. Rugs. Pencils and paper.

Even William.

Yet none of it moved. It all held perfectly still.

Rendal slowly turned around.

"You can bow to me now, Riley, or I will take more. I will take it slowly, like a tick drawing blood. But unlike a tick, the amount of blood I can hold is immeasurable. I'll take everything from you until there is literally nothing left. Is that what you want? Or will you join me?'

Riley felt her jaw relax. She could move it, enough to answer him at least.

"I'll die first."

"No, but everyone you love will. I'll tell you where I'm going first. To Sidnie. I'll conquer them, and I won't treat them nearly as kindly as I have Mason. They will suffer because' of your choice. After Sidnie, I'll come for New Perth. The longer you hold out, the more people will hurt. Him over there? William? I'll leave him for you now, but only because his pain will be worse later. You can stop it all by simply pledging your allegiance, Riley."

Riley felt a storm rising in her, the magic she'd sought for so long. It was coming up, and nothing could stop it.

"Good," he said. "Bring it forth and feel your rightful power."

Her eyes turned completely red and flames flowed from her fingers—the only things moving in this room. Still, Rendal's power held her suspended.

"Yes. Hate. Feel it. Embrace it," the mage whispered. "That was what I felt when they turned me from New Perth. It's what I feel now. Take it as your mantle too. I'll let Mason live, Riley. Take the hate and bow."

Riley closed her eyes, feeling this power inside her. It was still building, growing stronger as her rage increased.

"Yes. There it is. Bring it forth, child. Be my heir."

Riley's eyes flashed open, her powers cracking through

his.

She dropped to the floor, her left hand and entire sword blazing red. She swept across the floor, her sword a dazzling array of flames and smoke.

Riley brought it down, trying to slice straight through Rendal's collarbone. The mage's hand met it, mere inches separating the steel from his flesh. She pressed down, staring into the man's red eyes, but he pushed up with the edge of his hand, an inch of air between it and the blade.

Neither made a sound, but Riley felt his strength.

Unbelievable, she thought.

Yet, she saw him straining too. Struggling to hold her off.

Riley broke the stalemate, sweeping her sword around as she danced behind him. She brought it at his head, but her feet slipped out from under her.

She hit the floor hard, her face slamming into the wood. Her body was ripped backward and into the air so that she was flying again.

She collided with the wall as Rendal floated forward.

"Strength without skill, Riley. You can't win. You can't control it. You don't know what you're doing. That's okay, though. Through suffering comes enlightenment."

"Fuck you," she uttered, slicing at the mage. His left hand blocked the blade easily, slapping it away.

Every muscle in Riley's body struggled forward, but she couldn't break his hold. She watched angrily as Rendal's right hand moved up, palm facing her.

"See you soon, Right Hand."

He swiped his palm across her face, and Riley saw only darkness.

CHAPTER NINE

"R*ILEY!*"

William's call ripped Riley from the darkness.

Her body reacted without her command. She had no idea where she was, but whirled onto her stomach and then leapt to her feet, sword in hand.

"DAMN IT, RILEY!" William swayed on his feet. "We got to train you better, skinny. You couldn't handle that fuckin' old man any better than a toddler could've."

He put his hand to his head, giving her both a grimace and a smile.

Riley didn't understand what was happening. She stood on the docks, but they were alone. No ships or people, just her and William.

She turned to the jungle.

There was no more jungle.

Only the ashes and red embers of burned trees and buildings.

"What the hell happened?" she whispered to herself.

William stumbled across the docks, his footsteps loud in the otherwise deafening silence.

"I just told ya what the hell happened," he grumbled. "Ya lost *another* fight with him. I don't know how you keep losin'… Ugh, my head."

"Stop kidding around, William," Riley snapped. "Where's Mason? Where's the ship? Where's Rendal?"

"Slow down, girl." William sat on the ground. "What do you remember?"

Riley blinked, looking at the destroyed world in front of her. The island was in shambles, the buildings little more than flaming sticks.

"The group," Riley gasped, ignoring his question. "We've got to find out what happened to them."

William groaned but put his hand on the ground and pushed himself back up. "What I remember is me trying to caution us *against* going on that ship, and you pushin' the issue, so I'm blamin' *you* for this damned headache."

Riley rolled her eyes. "Later. We have to find Lucie and Worth. I don't see anyone, do you?"

William peered into the burning jungle. "No. No one."

Riley raced forward. Her head hurt horribly, but she had to see what had happened to her friends.

She moved much faster than when she'd come north last night because there was nothing in her way. William tried to keep up but fell farther behind.

Words from the night before came back to her slowly, floating through her head.

She tried to push them away.

Riley didn't have Mason, and now she might not have

the people that she'd come with. She might have lost everyone.

I'll take everything from you until there is literally nothing left.

Fuck that, her mind responded, and she focused on the path in front of her, her feet beating the ground rapidly.

She reached the building. Fire burned across the outside, the exterior black with ash.

A dead tree lay leaned on the building.

William caught up, his breathing ragged. "Damn it, Riley. I wish you had fought this hard last night. Maybe none of this would have happened."

She ignored the jab.

Riley heard and saw no one, simply witnessed the same destruction she'd seen on her way here.

The circular building's front door opened and Riley drew her sword from its sheath.

Worth stumbled out, and if it weren't for the chalice in his hand, Riley would have thought him injured.

That, and his purple lips.

"Twocuts. Great wine. Great, great wine."

He smiled broadly.

"Father and Mother," William swore. "This lout is drunk off his ass, and the entire island just burned down."

Hot, happy tears rushed to Riley's eyes. She didn't bother sheathing her sword, just ran forward and wrapped her arms around the big man.

"Where is everyone else? Are they okay?"

"Careful!" Worth shouted, backing up and staring into his chalice. "This good! Careful, Riley!" He glared at her.

"Oh, you damn fool!" she smiled as she pushed past him into the building.

She heard William yelling something behind her, but she paid no attention. Once inside, she stopped and looked across the interior.

They're here, she thought. *They're all here.*

Lucie, Erin, Verith—

"Eric? Where's Eric?" she shouted.

Everyone in the room was staring at her as if they couldn't believe their eyes.

"You're alive," Lucie whispered. "How is it possible?"

"Where is *Eric*?" Riley shouted.

"It's okay, Right Hand." Erin stepped forward and placed her hand on Riley's shoulder. "He's injured, but he's okay. Twocuts took him aboard his ship, and he's receiving care."

William entered the room.

"Oh, thank heavens," Lucie whispered but shut her mouth so quickly her teeth clicked together.

"No need to hide it, Lucie. I heard you. You're glad I'm alive." William smiled broadly. "And I'm never gonna let you live that down." He stepped deeper into the building, taking in his surroundings. His voice changed as he looked at Erin. "I'm very glad you're okay, my lady."

"Oh, cut the shit," Lucie said. "My lady this and my lady that. Everyone here can tell ya got the hots for her."

William flushed and quickly turned away from Erin.

"I'm glad you're okay too, Right Hand," Erin responded.

William acted like he didn't hear her and stared at Lucie with fresh anger. "What the hell happened here? I left to go kick ass, and when I wake up, everything's burnt to the ground."

"Thought both you dead, aye." Worth walked into the building. His eyes were bloodshot, and he was stumbling much worse than usual. "Said, betcha, both dead."

"Where is everyone?" Riley asked. "Where are the rest of our troops?"

"You should sit down, Riley." Verith stepped toward her from the side of the room.

"Hell, no! Tell me what the fuck happened!"

The room fell silent beneath Riley's rage.

Nearly a minute that silence stretched, then Lucie spoke.

"Fire. It came from Rendal's ship. I saw it with my mind, and so did Worth—"

"Aye," Worth agreed. "Saw it, Worth did."

"It flowed from the ship, barreling right out," Lucie continued. "It didn't stop either, like fire should. It kept flowing, catching everything in its wake."

Again, the silence.

"A lot of people died, Riley. A lot of pirates. A lot of our people. A lot of Worth's people."

Worth threw his chalice against the wall. The metal dented, and purple wine splashed across the stone wall. "Aye. He killed Worth people. He killed lots of Worth people."

Riley knew what that meant to him, because unlike the citizens of New Perth, Worth didn't have a lot of people. His tent city had numbered perhaps eighty, and each time they ventured out with Riley, more died.

Worth collapsed and leaned against the wall. He put his hands on his face and sobbed silently into them.

Verith kept talking, doing his best to ignore the mourning man. "Lucie and Worth kept us safe. Their combined power formed a shield around the building, although the fire pushed closer and closer, as you can tell from looking at the outside. It never got in, though."

Erin spoke next. "A lot of pirates died. Those who didn't took to the sea early this morning. If you walk to the south end of the island, you can see their ships. Eric's with them. They have better medicine."

"What are they doing?"

"They're having a parley and deciding what to do," Erin answered.

"With who?"

"First, with us," Erin said. "Secondly, about Rendal."

"With us?" William spoke up. "I'll tell them what they can do with us: come here and let me cut them down one by one. What the hell are they talkin' about?"

"We're not pirates, and we're on the sea. Our ships are still intact. By ocean law, they can kill us and take our property if we're not strong enough to defend it."

Riley pulled away from both of them. She walked to a chair sitting at one of the tables and sat down.

"Everyone, just hold on." Riley closed her eyes. "It doesn't matter what they're doing. They're not going to attack us."

"And how can ya be so sure, skinny?"

She looked up, grinning. "All that brawn, and not many brains. For one, they took Eric to help him heal. I don't see that as an act of aggression, do you?"

William's eyes narrowed, but he remained quiet.

"Exactly. They're not going to kill us. And even if they tried, it's not a guaranteed thing—unless you're scared to face the pirates, chubby?"

"More like they're scared to face *me*," William retorted.

"Good." Riley turned her head to her feet and closed her eyes again. "Do you remember what happened last night, William? We need to focus on Rendal right now. I know the loss of people is painful for everyone, myself included, but if we want to avenge them, we have to stop the mage. Do you remember what happened?"

"Not a lot," William admitted. "I remember trying to attack him, and then I couldn't breathe. That's the end of it until I woke up on the docks."

"But you said I'd lost a fight. That made it sound like you had watched." Riley looked at him.

"Just givin' ya shit." William grinned.

"You mean to tell me, when you awoke from nearly being killed by a dark mage, the first thing you thought about was fucking with me?"

"Aye." William chuckled. "What can I say? I'm an asshole."

Riley rolled her eyes. "You're ridiculous. Some of what happened is coming back to me. The important parts, and that's what Rendal told me. He said he's going to take everything away from me slowly until I join him."

"Then why didn't he kill *me*?" William asked.

"He knows I don't care about you." Riley grinned. She wasn't going to tell William what Rendal had said. Not right now, at least.

"He knows you'd be lost without me, skinny," William shot back.

Riley kept going. "He told me he's going to Sidnie to destroy it."

"That's impossible," Verith spoke up. "I've been to Sidnie. Has anyone else?"

Everyone stared at the general, shaking their heads *no*.

"I went as a young man. Even then, it dwarfed New Perth, and I'm not speaking ill of my own kingdom. I love New Perth, but Sidnie is something unto itself. He can't take it. I don't care what magic he possesses."

"That was what he told me," Riley answered. "He's going there."

"You sure that mage didn't knock your head a bit too hard?" William asked.

"No harder than I'm about to knock yours. That was what he said," Riley answered.

"He can do it." Lucie spoke now. "If he says he can, then he can. I felt him last night; I have a close connection to him, even after all these years."

Riley glanced at William, knowing he would want to make some kind of crude comment. He was grinning but caught her look. He winked and kept his mouth shut.

"He's stronger than any of us can imagine. That fire last night…it shouldn't have been possible, yet it wiped out the entire island. Everyone but us, and I think he left us here for a reason."

Riley closed her eyes, remembering what Rendal had said.

I'll take everything from you until there is literally nothing left.

And that he was going to do it slowly.

These people here with her—they mattered to Riley, so he'd left them for later.

Riley looked at Verith. "We have to assume he's telling the truth. We have to assume he's going there, and he'll do what he said…and he still has Mason."

"Did you see Mason?" Verith asked.

Riley shook her head. "We never got close enough."

"'Cause you didn't let me kick his ass like I wanted." William had a sly look on his face. "If you'd have stepped aside, we'd all be safe and at New Perth by now."

"If I'd stepped aside, we'd probably all be wearing green or red necklaces." She turned to Verith. "We have to get to Sidnie."

"It'll be easier with ships. We're nearly halfway around the continent as is, and we won't have to deal with the Badlands," Verith responded. "We'll need to determine how many men short we are to run the ships—"

"None," Erin interrupted. "Not with our ship."

"Well, then I suppose we can leave as soon as you want, Riley," Verith finished.

"No."

Everyone in the room looked at Worth.

"What?" William said.

"No. We no go Sidnie," Worth answered.

"Why not?" William asked.

"She no ready. I told you before. She no ready." Worth looked at Riley. "You need train. You need time. Need focus."

Riley felt exasperated, unable to explain to this man that they didn't have *time.*

"He has the person I serve, Worth. He's going to *kill* other people right now because of my decision not to join him. There isn't time to do what you're asking of me. There just isn't. We have to go forward."

"So dumb." Worth wasn't smiling. His lips were purple, but his face was like an ancient gargoyle's. "Dumb! You lose. Every time. He win. Every time. Because you no *slow down*. You chase all over world. Here, there, wherever he point. You like pet. You need listen to Worth."

He stood up surprisingly easily for someone of his weight and level of drunkenness. He looked at William.

"Listen. She no go. You go. You all go. You see what mage do, and you try stop him. Sneaky-like. Not full frontal assault. Riley. Her and Worth, we go train."

William didn't give a ridiculous retort but actually seemed to be considering the man's words.

"No." Riley stood. "I'm not letting anyone go in my stead."

"Hush, Riley," William whispered.

"No! You aren't going to tell me what the fuck I'm going to do!" she shouted.

William turned to her, his face soft—no jokes in him now. "Hey, just hear me out. Listen to what I'm about to say and *then* tell me what you think, okay?"

Riley's face was hot, and she wanted to rip down the entire building. Her hands were fisted, but she only nodded.

"Worth is right, at least about some of this. We *are* chasing him around. We *do* go wherever he is, even out into the ocean, which isn't New Perth's way. We keep doing the same thing over and over, and it ain't workin'."

He glanced at Lucie. "You might think I'm dumb, but I ain't."

He turned back to Riley. "Rendal is leadin' us by the nose, skinny, and if you let go of your pride and your sense of duty for a second, you'll see it. Why do you think he told you he was goin' to Sidnie? Because he wanted you to chase him there like a dog chases a rabbit."

Riley's hands relaxed some.

"Despite my clearly badass powers, I don't know much about magic." William winked before continuing, "Worth does, though. He knows magic, and he has lost as much as anyone in this. You know what I *ain't* hear him say a moment ago? He ain't say he was done. That he was takin' his people back to the desert. He said you and he need to get to work, skinny. He's in this, but he's wantin' to do it the smart way. You're not. You want Rendal to keep playin' ya."

Riley took a deep breath, steadying herself. "What exactly are you saying, William?"

"Sheesh, Lucie. This girl is as dumb as you." William grinned. "I'm sayin' you go with Worth. Wherever he wants to take you. You learn, and when I see you again, you use all this magic everyone says you got. The rest of us, we'll go to Sidnie. We'll go undercover, and we'll find out exactly what the prick is up to."

Riley looked at Lucie. "What do you think?"

She nodded. "Worth is right. You can't beat Rendal yet, and he's using you. You need to learn. You need to dedicate yourself to magic, not think only of savin' Mason."

"Verith," Riley asked, "can you get everyone into the city?"

He looked at William. "I don't know. Big man, can you be inconspicuous?"

"In-con-whatuous?" William responded.

Verith smiled and looked at Riley. "We'll be all right."

Finally, Riley went back to Worth. "Where are we going? Back to New Perth?"

Worth laughed, his usual jolly demeanor returning for a moment. "New Perth have no magic. We go Badlands. Underground people."

"Under what?" William's eyebrows raised high.

"Underground people. They show her. They teach her. We go there."

Erin stepped forward. "I want Eric to go with you. I want him to keep learning."

Riley raised her eyebrows and looked at Worth. "That's up to you."

"Eric fine. He good student. Not like you." Worth, surprisingly, hadn't dropped his grin.

Riley laughed. She didn't know what else to do. Her life had changed so much in the past few weeks that she nearly couldn't recognize it, yet the only choice was to go forward. To meet these challenges with clear eyes and a full heart.

"Okay, Worth. To the underground people we go." She looked at William. "Two things: don't you or anyone else here get killed."

"What's the second?" William asked.

"If you try to kiss Erin while we're gone, don't blush too bad."

William's entire faced turned the color of an apple.

CHAPTER TEN

Brighten Alanon saw the ships before anyone else. He saw them because his eyes were sharper than anyone he'd ever met, and although he was only fifteen, he thought them probably sharper than anyone in all of Sidnie. Truth be told, he thought both his eyes and ears were the sharpest in the whole kingdom.

"What the fuck is that?" he asked Kris.

"What's what?"

Kris was the same age as Brighten, and they'd known each other for as long as either could remember.

"Them ships out there. Ya don't see 'em?"

"Hell no, I don't see 'em. Why you think I hang out with you, Brighten? Because your personality is so good? I'm here because you're the best lookout in the city."

Brighten punched her in the shoulder, a light thing because he hadn't taken his eyes off the ships.

Brighten and Kris lived on the streets, and right now they were sitting on top of one of Sidnie's condemned buildings. Most other people would have been far too frightened to climb up to the roof, but Brighten and Kris knew Sidnie's underbelly like they knew themselves.

They understood every false step on nearly every roof in the city.

"That's too many ships," Brighten whispered.

And it was. Sidnie had a port and ships came and went, but never this many, and never in a line like that.

"How many?" Kris asked without looking up from her game of cards.

"Ten."

Kris *did* look up then. "Quit lyin', boy, or I'mma beat you blue. There ain't ten ships comin' this way."

"You'll hear sirens soon." Brighten was hardly paying attention to his friend. He couldn't pull his eyes from the ships. "This isn't normal."

He stood up.

"Whadda we do?" Kris asked, standing up and forgetting about the cards.

"Hell if I know."

"Boys are idiots," Kris snapped. "Come on. We need to get away from the port."

The two left the top of the building, racing down the streets they knew so well.

"Where ya goin'?" another street urchin called to them.

"Run!" Brighten shouted back.

"Have you ever seen Sidnie before?" Rendal asked.

The sun hurt Mason's eyes. He hadn't seen it in long days, having been kept below in the cages. He was dirty and exhausted, but he knew he had it better than the other people he'd seen. They were being *drained*.

"No," he answered the mage.

"It's really something, isn't it?"

Mason had to admit, even if only privately, that the mage was correct.

The city spread out before him, large towers jutting into the sky. Its buildings dwarfed New Perth's, and Mason found himself amazed that they could construct such things.

Reading his mind, Rendal said, "They used magic—the same magic New Perth refused."

A siren was blaring.

"They're gathering their military." Rendal stood at Mason's side, no grin on his face. Mason didn't know what kind of magic he was using, but the mage's eyes were red. "They've spotted us, and we're both a large force and unexpected. They'll be ready for battle by the time we get there."

"A city that size…" Mason's voice trailed off, and he gazed at the mage. "You're going insane. Do you realize that? You're losing your mind."

Rendal still didn't smile. His face was focused. "No, I'm not. You may be right in what you're thinking, though. A city of that size would be very difficult to overtake, even given my powers and my army, but I won't be doing it by brute force, my dear Mason."

"What are you going to do?"

"I'll show you when I'm finished," the mage answered. "Harold, please take our guest back down."

Harold grabbed Mason roughly and pulled him away.

Rendal stood alone on the deck. He was only partially

there, though—only his body remained. His mind was in Sidnie, watching the military scramble to ready itself.

Sidnie's Prefect was coming down from his tower, his aides having alerted him to what was going on in his kingdom.

Rendal had heard of the man—Sidnie's Prefect. His name was Lawrence Slidell, and he was newly ascended.

Sidnie's Prefect *had* to be proficient with magic, and usually was the greatest user in the kingdom. They had actually followed through with Rendal's plan without knowing it.

Rendal couldn't gain access to the man's mind without alerting him to his own power. Rendal had no doubt that he *could* infiltrate the Prefect, but as he told Mason, this wasn't a brute-force mission.

Harold returned from jailing Mason.

"Sir, what would you have me do next?"

"I'm commanding the other ships to remain at this distance and go no closer to shore. Only ours is going forward. I want you to let the men on board know that. Also, they're going to inspect the ship, without a doubt. Under no circumstances is anyone to make it to the cages. You understand?"

"I do, sir. No one will see them," Harold answered.

Rendal's eyes returned to their normal color. "Good. We'll arrive in the next thirty minutes. Prepare the ship, and meet me on deck."

"Sir?" Harold was perplexed.

"Yes. You're coming with me. I'm a merchant, those ships out there are mine, and I've come to Sidnie personally because I want to start a favorable relationship with them." Rendal smiled and looked at Harold. "You're my accountant."

"Accountant?" Harold asked.

"How are you with numbers?"

"I'm better with my sword."

Rendal laughed. "Indeed you are! Tell me, Harold, do you think you could kill William? The other Right Hand?"

"I believe I could, yes," Harold answered.

Rendal turned again, his smile fading. "That's what I wanted to hear. I hope you'll get a chance to prove yourself right soon. Be ready, Harold, because that man is dangerous. If you fail, I don't think you'll have to answer to me."

He smiled once again.

"Because you'll be dead."

***

Worth wore a large pack on his back.

Riley had almost throttled the bald man when she found out what was in it, but then she'd just started laughing.

She hadn't been able to help it.

Rather than packing provisions and weapons and other survival gear, the man had lined the pack with leather and filled it to the brim with wine.

"Twocut's wine good. Too good to leave. Worth take."

The pirate had let him have it, saying "I stole it off some merchant. Pirates don't drink the shit."

Worth was happy with that, and to his credit, he wasn't stone-drunk as they crossed through the desert.

Riley and Eric were both clothed from head to toe to

keep the sun from blistering them. Worth looked the same as always, his bald head deep brown and needing very little protection from the elements.

This is his home, Riley thought.

William and the crew had dropped them off a day ago. No tears, but lots of hugs and handshakes, nearly everyone unsure if they would see each other again.

They'd traveled in silence for a long time today, and it was nearing noon. Worth walked in front, stopping briefly to refill his chalice from time to time but otherwise forging onward.

Riley was impressed that Worth never spilled the wine, walking in all this sand.

She followed him, and Eric followed her.

Riley was tired of not knowing what the hell was going on, though, so she jogged forward and caught up with Worth.

"Who are these people?"

The bald man didn't turn as he spoke, his eyes narrow and staring straight forward. "Underground people."

"You keep saying that, Worth, but I don't know what the hell that means. Do they actually live *underground* or is that a metaphor?"

"Worth no know metaphor," he answered.

"Do they live beneath the sand? Is that what you're telling me?"

"Yes. That what Worth telling you." He grinned, and Riley understood he was mocking her.

She grinned back. "Hush. How do they live underground? Is that even possible?"

Worth shrugged. "I never ask."

"How do you know them?" Riley said.

"Everyone in Badlands know of 'em."

It was a delicate difference, but Riley caught it. "Wait, you don't actually know them?"

Worth shook his head. "They underground. Worth above ground. When we meet?" He sounded as if this should be apparent.

"Well, where are they?"

Another shrug. "Worth no know."

"Worth! How are we supposed to get there if you don't know them or where they are?" Riley could hardly believe what he was saying.

"They know we here. They contact." He spoke as if he had no concerns at all.

"How?"

"Too many questions. Know that?" Worth glanced at her, clearly annoyed.

Riley glanced behind her at Eric. The young man's face was covered so she couldn't tell if he had heard anything, but she doubted Eric missed much.

"How will they know we're here?" she asked, turning back to Worth.

"You not so quick in desert, aye?"

"Huh?" Riley asked, right before she smelled them. Her head whipped up, looking toward the new scent.

"Out here, my place." Worth smiled. "You smell them, betcha."

She did. The wind was blowing toward them, and she was shocked that Worth had known these strangers were here before she did. Her senses were *always* first in class.

She scanned the desert, and she thought she could just

see something in the distance, although it was hard to tell. The sun caused everything to waver like a mirage.

"Is it the underground people?" she asked. She hadn't drawn her sword yet; they were too far away for that.

"No. What come before underground people."

"And who the hell is that, Worth?" Riley snapped.

Worth smiled wide. "Raiders."

"Oh, great," Riley responded, shaking her head. "Ya know, Worth, it might have helped me make my decision if you'd told me everything we would be facing *before* we faced it. I might have just decided to chase Rendal."

"Then where fun at?" He laughed.

She grinned. In reality, she was itching for a fight, especially after what had happened with Rendal. She didn't like losing, and while she hadn't *technically* lost against the mage, she hadn't won either.

Riley wasn't scared of Badlands raiders. On the coast they were called bandits, and Riley had regularly cut them down like a blade does wheat.

"What do we do?"

Worth shook his head. "You simple, Riley. Magic, yes, but simple. We wait. They come to us."

Riley opened her mouth to say something, but Worth shook his head. "Enough question. Let Worth have peace!"

He walked faster, and Riley couldn't help but laugh at the man.

They went on for another hour, and Riley caught the raiders' scent every now and then. She was surprised to be able to smell them, especially at such a distance, but she knew it was true.

It wasn't a *bad* smell per se, but an odd one.

Something she hadn't smelled before.

Finally, Worth came to a stop without saying anything. Both Riley and Eric walked to him and then halted.

"One, we protect wine. Raider no get wine, understand?"

He looked at them with a seriousness Riley rarely saw from the man. She wanted to laugh but thought he might take offense. He wasn't playing games about his booze.

"Sure, Worth. We'll both die for the wine if that's what you want," she answered. "Why are we stopping, though? I still don't see anyone."

"You never make it in Badlands, Right Hand. You too soft."

"He's right, little lady."

The voice came from nowhere. Riley's sword was out of its sheath and in her hand before the voice finished.

"No move," Worth said. "Stay."

Riley saw that Eric's sword was clear, too, though no fire covered it yet.

"Go ahead and put the weapons down," the voice spoke again. It was strangely mechanical but sounded like a man's.

The smell had grown stronger too.

About ten feet in front of her Riley saw green stones, what Erin called amphoralds. They seemed to appear from nowhere and hung right in the middle of the air, attached to nothing.

"What is that?" she whispered harshly.

"*No move.*" Worth's face was grim.

More green amphoralds lit up in a circle around them, and Riley was finally able to make sense of the smell.

Something's burning, she thought.

"Weapons *down!*" the mechanical voice shouted, though it was more human now.

"I don't drop my weapon for anyone, let alone a ghost," Riley shot back.

The world around her shimmered slightly; it made Riley nauseated for a second.

The shimmering grew in intensity, then quit all at once.

Twelve men and women surrounded the three of them.

Worth smiled. "That okay. Not too many." He looked at Riley. "They no magic. They just pretend."

"What the hell does that matter, Worth?"

He smiled bigger. "It matter. They *no* magic. *We* magic."

"Enough with the talk," the man in front commanded. "Put the fuckin' blades on the ground and give us your packs."

The one talking was heavily muscled. Riley quickly flashed glances at the others. They were all thinner but looked at be in decent shape. These people weren't starving to death.

Riley didn't understand how they had simply *appeared*, but she also didn't have time right now. There was ass to be kicked.

"Eric." Worth was smiling since he could see the raiders. "Put sword down." The bald man proceeded to sit down in the sand, folding his legs under him. He looked at Eric. The kid wasn't putting *shit* down.

Worth sighed. His eyes lit red for a second and the sword flew into the ground, burying itself hilt-deep in the sand.

"What the hell are you doing, Worth?" Riley growled. She didn't take her eyes from the raiders.

"Eric, come. Sit with Worth." The bald man sounded actually *happy*.

Riley swallowed, not sure what in the hell was happening. Was Worth a traitor? Had he made some deal with these raiders to bring them a woman? Some sick vengeance for what happened to his people?

"Eric. Sit, boy. Sit with Worth. This be fun. Lots and lots." Worth took his pack off and put it in front of him. He opened the top, carefully dipped his chalice, and closed the pack. His smile dropped away, and he looked at Riley. "*Remember.* No harm to wine."

He smiled.

"Eric! Sit!"

The young man lost his mask of death, appearing confused instead. He glanced at Riley, wanting for her approval.

"What the fuck?" she said aloud, deciding whether to trust Worth. She supposed she had to. "Go ahead; do what the drunk tells you."

"ENOUGH!" the raider shouted. "I don't know what the fuck is going on here, but ya better start listenin' or we're just gonna cut ya up! Put the fuckin' sword *down*!"

Riley's mind let go of Worth and his ridiculous behavior. It let go of Eric and everything else. It focused only on the coming carnage, and the killer in her ignited.

"How about I put it down your throat instead?"

The rest of the raiders looked confused. They hadn't expected the mage sitting in the sand, and now a woman faced them with a sword.

The head raider looked to his right and then his left. "I'm tryin' to figure out exactly what's happenin' here, but I guess it don't really matter. Since ya won't put the sword down, I suppose we'll have a go atcha once we disarm ya. Ladies, any of y'all want either of these two men to bring home?"

"Aye," one of them said. "I'll take the young 'un and add 'im to my collection."

"No one wants the drunk?" the raider asked.

"Just kill 'em," someone said. "Tired of all this talk."

"Aye, me too," the head raider responded.

"Then quit talking," Riley snapped, "and come get me."

The ones behind her came first, as Riley had expected. One swung for her head, but she ducked, spun, and drove her sword through his back. One came from her left; she wrenched the sword free and drew it across the woman's stomach.

Both raiders screamed, but the fighting was only beginning.

Worth smiled broadly and took a sip from his chalice.

More were coming at her now, more than she could see. She dodged their blows, parrying and striking like a possessed serpent. Her reaction time was twice as fast as that of anyone coming for her, but there were too many.

Loud *clangs* of metal hitting metal mixed with the screams of the dying.

Too many, she thought. Sand kicked up from her heels as she danced around her foes.

Riley felt a sword slash close to her robe—far too close. She swung her blade around and caught the man across the throat.

She barely saw the shield.

It hit her in the back and sent her sprawling across the sand. She quickly tried to regain her feet, but the sand betrayed her and she fell to her knees.

She looked up. They were nearly on her. Eight of them, their weapons pointed at her. They wouldn't take any chances with "having a go"; Riley knew that. She was too dangerous. They were going to kill her and take whatever valuables she possessed.

She could kill maybe three, but not all of them. No way.

Just before they fell on her, she looked at Worth.

He smiled broadly and nodded.

Go on. You magic. His voice filled her head.

Red color ripped across Riley's pupils, the rising tide inside her bursting forth. She shrieked in anger, knowing it was her last chance. They were on her.

A wave rolled out from Riley, although it couldn't be seen immediately. Wind rushed at the oncoming attackers, ruffling their clothes and hair.

Then it hit them.

All eight flew into the air, ten feet high, then twenty, thirty, fifty, a hundred.

Riley stared up at them as they rose higher and higher.

The red in her eyes died, and they started to drop. She heard their screams, distant as they were.

They fell to the ground, arms and legs flailing as if it might save them.

The ground stopped their screams.

"Good." Worth clapped his hands. "Now underground people come."

Riley jumped to her feet holding her sword, rage on her

face. "YOU ALMOST GOT ME KILLED! NEITHER OF YOU HELPED!"

Worth looked at Eric. "She worry too much, aye?"

Eric smiled. "Aye, definitely does."

"Sit," Worth told her happily. "We wait. Underground people come."

Riley wanted to hit them on their heads with her hilt, but she slowly got control of her breathing. The people she'd killed were lying in the sand, no longer making noise, and she stepped over them as she came toward Worth.

She didn't sit down, though. "Why was that necessary?"

"Let underground people know we here. Need big magic. Little no good."

"I could have…" Her voice trailed off. Worth was simply looking forward and taking a sip of his wine. She could yell at him all she wanted, but he wouldn't give a damn.

And she was alive.

She turned to Eric, hoping to loose some of her anger on him. "And what about you? You didn't help either."

Eric looked away, ashamed. "He was in my head. He said you would be fine. I… I'm sorry."

"Twelve on one, and I was going to be fine?"

"Well…" Eric grew silent for a moment and looked at the dead bodies. "They're all dead, and you *are* fine."

Riley followed his gaze.

The young man smiled, still staring. "I sorta feel bad for 'em. They didn't stand a chance."

Riley couldn't hold back her smile either. "Maybe you're right."

"'Course Worth right," the tent man interrupted. "Worth always right. Now just wait. Always questions."

He shook his head and took a large swig of his wine.

An hour passed…and nothing changed.

"Worth, this is getting ridicu—" Riley didn't get the chance to finish her sentence.

The ground beneath her shook, the sand vibrating under her body. In front of her, she saw a *wave*. It made no sense—none at all—but that was what she saw. A wave, as if she were on the ocean.

And it was growing larger.

Stretching high into the sky, growing taller with each passing second. A hundred feet in the air now.

Riley jumped up, with Eric only moments behind. Worth didn't move.

"Hey… Hey, Worth, buddy. We gotta go. We gotta go right now." Riley swallowed. She didn't think there was any possible chance of outrunning this *thing*, but they had to try.

"Sit, sit." Worth patted the vibrating sand, smiling.

Riley whipped toward him, grabbing him by his arms. She pulled, lifting him easily despite his weight. He was on his feet in only a second, not prepared at all for such action.

Riley started dragging him, but Worth fought back, trying to hold himself in place.

The shaking was growing worse.

"WORTH! IT'S COMING! LET'S GO!"

Worth shook his head and only stared at the oncoming sand tsunami. "Calm, woman. Calm. Everything okay. Too much worry."

It was hard to hear him because the rumbling ground was making too much noise.

The wave was nearly on them, and there wasn't anywhere to run.

Riley faced the unstoppable sand. If she weren't going to survive, she'd meet death honorably.

It reached them in mere seconds, and Riley closed her eyes, bracing for unbelievable pain.

It didn't come. She didn't feel the abrasive sand hitting her, nor was she knocked off her feet.

She opened her eyes and found herself staring at a thin man.

Riley didn't raise her sword to protect her. Didn't move at all, actually.

The man's eyes were gray and dim. He was old, much older than anyone Riley had ever seen, except perhaps Rendal.

"Who are you?" he asked, looking at Riley.

"Muh-my name is Riley Trident." It was the first time she could remember stuttering, if only briefly.

"Well, speak clearly then, Riley Trident," the man said. "We do not allow stutterers where I come from."

Worth looked at Riley and grinned. "He funny."

"And you are?" the old man asked.

"I Worth. That Eric." Worth tilted his head toward the young man.

"Did you mean to summon me? Answer me true. I'll be able to tell if not."

Worth put his bag on the ground, seeming to ignore the man's question. He opened it, dipped his chalice again, and closed the bag before looking at the old man.

"'Course Worth did. Need speak to queen."

The old man's eyes narrowed. "Why do you think she'll speak to you?"

"Look." Worth titled his head to Riley. "See yourself."

The man did as Worth told him, staring at Riley. The Right Hand was silent.

"You see." Worth nodded.

"Maybe. Maybe you're right, but that's a long way from being definitely right. Many have potential."

Riley didn't look away from the man as she spoke. "What the hell is going on, Worth?"

He shook his head. "Always so many questions." He looked at the stranger as if he might understand.

The gray-eyed man showed no emotion.

"Queen want to see her, betcha." Worth's smile was wide.

"Perhaps." The gray-eyed man nodded as if making a decision. He looked at Worth and Eric. "You two are what, then? If she's here for the queen, why are *you* here?"

"We friends. We go if she go. Otherwise," Worth shook his head, "no."

The man eyed Worth but then nodded again. "So be it. Come."

With that, he turned around and started walking. He said nothing else, and his pace was harsh right out of the gate.

"Worth, if you don't tell me what is going on right now, I'm going to break your kneecaps and leave you out here to die under this sun." Riley didn't move an inch. She stared at Worth.

"Underground people." Worth smiled as he stared at the man walking into the distance. He brought his index finger to his temple and twirled it. "A little crazy, they. It help us, though. They *big* magic. Come. Let's go."

Worth started, the big man—now somewhat drunk—easily keeping up with the gray-eyed man.

Riley looked at Eric, who only shrugged.

"A lot of help you've been today," Riley quipped, then followed Worth.

She didn't know how long they walked, but the pace was grueling. Worth handled it fine, but Riley found she was walking too fast to ask any more questions—which Worth probably *loved*.

Finally, the stranger stopped. He held a staff in his right hand—a gnarled piece of wood that looked at least as old as him.

He waited until the group caught up to him and then banged his staff three times on the sand.

Riley jumped back.

The sand started swirling where his staff touched it. Small at first, but growing bigger, and then Riley realized what was happening.

Her breath caught in her throat.

The ground was sinking.

Riley glanced at Worth, but he only put a single finger to his purple lips.

"Shhhh."

The sand swirled up and around her, yet *she* wasn't sinking.

She froze in place, and suddenly she saw how beautiful it was—the sand swirling around her as if she were caught up in some benign tornado.

The stranger's eyes had turned from gray to red, and

Riley slowly started descending as the sand continued to swirl.

She looked at Worth. He held his chalice in one hand, and had the other over its top, keeping any sand from flying in.

Riley looked below her and saw a door opening, along with someone staring up from beneath. The door swung *upward*, and Riley's group descended through it.

A woman snapped it closed as Riley landed on solid metal.

The stranger's eyes turned back to gray.

A second passed, then Riley heard *and* felt the sand collapse again. The tunnel she now stood in shook.

"What do they want?" the new woman asked.

The male stranger looked at Riley. "Her. It's possible. They want to see the queen."

"Hold on," Riley interrupted. "Everyone just hold the hell on for a second. Who are you two, and where are we?"

The strangers both looked at her.

"I'm Thomas," the man said.

The woman followed with, "I'm Rachel."

"Do you have last names?" Riley asked, wanting it all out at once.

"No. The Chosen don't have last names. There's no need," Thomas said.

Riley looked at Worth. "The Chosen?"

Worth shrugged, taking his hand off his chalice. "Underground people."

"That's what those above call us." The man sneered. "It's derogatory, and you'll refrain from using it while you're down here. You're our guests. Don't forget that."

Riley nodded. "That's fine. The Chosen. Now, *where* is this place?"

Rachel spoke next. "The Elders built this place."

Riley knew some of the Elders, although not a lot. They were the people from before the world began again.

The two strangers started walking as if that had answered the whole question.

"No, no." Riley passed both of them easily and halted, stopping them in their tracks. "I've got a lot of questions. What is *this*?"

"Told you." Worth smiled from behind. "'Lotta questions. Always."

"*We* can walk and talk," Rachel commented. "Can you?"

The man didn't wait but simply brushed by Riley and kept moving forward.

Rachel followed suit.

"Not the friendliest folks, huh, Worth?"

He shook his head. "Nope. Underground people rude."

"I heard that!" Thomas called.

The three started walking. "All right," Riley said. "We're doing half, you do the other half and start talking."

"The Elders built these tunnels long ago, we think as military bases, but no one can be sure. They were lost to humanity for a long time after the world was born again, until *she* found them."

"And who's she?" Riley asked.

"The first queen," Thomas answered. "Her name was Stephanie. Her daughter is our queen now, Alexandria."

"She reopened the halls. She brought us here and gave us a home, and now we wait for our savior," Rachel said.

Riley looked at Worth. He only twirled his finger at his temple again and mouthed the word, "Crazy."

Riley shut up, understanding that whatever these two were saying, she wasn't going to get anything else out of them that made sense. They spoke in reverent tones and truly believed whatever nonsense they were spouting.

Riley slowed down to open some space between the strangers.

"Worth, what are you getting us into?" she whispered.

"Questions. Always questions," he retorted, rolling his eyes. "They crazy but they help. You see. Just wait. Youthful. Impatient."

They walked in silence for a few minutes, passing hallways on their left and right. The place truly was large, and Riley didn't understand any of it.

She saw no one else as they went.

"You won't see them, either," Rachel spoke, clearly reading Riley's mind. "Not unless we want you too. You're here because you have potential, but that's all. Many people have potential."

"Worth?" Riley whispered, wishing she'd never agreed to any of this. She'd rather be with William and Verith than these people.

"You're welcome to leave whenever you want," Rachel retorted. "I *personally* don't think you're the one, but Thomas is right—you have potential."

"Stay *out* of my head," Riley shot back.

They reached another metal door. Thomas stopped and looked back at Riley. "She's in there."

"What? Just like that? Does she know I'm here?"

Worth touched Riley's elbow. "Please. Trust Worth. Go."

"They're coming with me," Riley told the two strangers.

Thomas shook his head. "No, they're not. You will go in alone, or you won't go in at all."

Riley looked at Worth. She hated this because she didn't understand it. "You two will be safe?"

"*Riley*," Eric stressed.

She looked at him, surprised. He'd unwrapped his head so she could see him now. There was no fear on his face, and none on Worth's either.

She knew why Eric wasn't afraid. He could kill everyone in here at the drop of a hat. And Worth understood what was going on.

She was the only one who felt fear, but it was for *their* safety.

"Get your ass in there," Eric said. "We can take care of ourselves, I fuckin' promise."

She laughed, breaking through the anxiety in her mind.

"I forget I'm traveling with killers." She looked at the two strangers. "Take me to her."

CHAPTER ELEVEN

A day had passed since the ship arrived at Sidnie.

Brighten watched it come to the dock, and then watched as two men strode off it. The military had surrounded them, although no one was killed.

They led the two men off while soldiers boarded the ship. The other nine ships remained offshore.

Brighten and Kris observed it all.

"What the fuck is goin' on?" Kris asked.

"You think I'm a mind reader? I don't know. I'm seeing the same things you are," Brighten responded.

"No, what I think is *next* time we steal some bread, I'm goin' to rat on you to the guards, and getcha put in jail. How about that?" She grinned at her friend.

They were waiting near the docks again, having just grabbed a few loaves from a merchant down the street. Brighten had been the lookout while Kris' quick hands did the dirty work. Now they were shoving the loot in their faces.

The other ships Brighten spotted yesterday sat in the

distance and the one that actually arrived remained mostly undisturbed. Some guards came and went from it—checking things or just fucking with the people inside, Brighten didn't know. Neither would surprise him. He didn't have fond feelings toward the guards, that was for sure.

Brighten heard the footsteps before he felt the hand, knowing that somehow he'd been snuck up on—and almost unable to believe it.

The hand that grabbed him by the neck changed all that, though. Brighten was wrenched off the ground, and he looked down immediately at Kris.

She had always been faster than he and was already bolting forward.

Another hand snapped out like a snake and grabbed her by the back of her shirt.

"Not a word," someone whispered harshly, and Brighten said nothing.

Not as physically quick as Kris, his mind worked super-fast. This wasn't a guard; they didn't whisper. It wasn't the merchant they'd stolen the bread from, because he didn't have the physical prowess to sneak up on Brighten. And finally, it wasn't anyone from the street, because Brighten knew all of them.

Kris, on the other hand, hadn't thought of all that and started shouting.

"Shut it, girl!" the man whispered a bit louder. "Right now or I'll break ya!"

"*SHUT THE FUCK UP AND LET GO OF ME!*" Kris shrieked, trying to wiggle out of the man's large hands.

"Verith!" the man said, his voice growing louder. "Help me with this little bitch!"

Brighten heard other footsteps now.

A man grabbed Kris and put his hand over her mouth. She tried biting him, but he clamped her jaw shut.

"William, I told ya those weren't the two to grab." A woman's voice now. "You make even worse decisions now that Riley's not here. Father and Mother, I wish she'd return!"

The woman walked in front of the two men and looked at Brighten and Kris.

"He's an oaf, and I apologize for it. We mean ya no harm, neither of ya."

She was older, short and stocky with a hard face. But her eyes were kind.

"Truth be told, we need yer help, but the oaf who's got hold of ya there said ya'd just run." The woman cast a harsh glance at the man holding Brighten. "If he puts ya down, will ya just hear me out?"

Kris had stopped struggling. *She* could get away if they put her down—most likely. The big man who held Brighten had to be fast as hell, given how easily he'd grabbed them.

"Yeah, I won't run," Brighten said.

"You think I'mma trust him, Lucie? You're dumber than you look," the big man grumbled.

She glared at him. "We're supposed to trust these kids. That's why we frickin' grabbed 'em, ain't it? If we can't trust what they tell us, we're gonna get killed. Now put him down!"

The old woman stomped her foot.

The big man hesitated for a moment but then lowered Brighten to the ground and let go of his neck.

"What about me?" Kris said, although her voice was muffled by the man holding her.

"Put her down, Verith," the old woman told him.

He did, and Kris did exactly what Brighten thought.

She *bolted*, legs pumping.

"Aw, damn it!" the big man said. He didn't move, though, probably thinking it wasn't worth the trouble. "I told you!"

Kris stopped about ten feet away.

She turned around and found Brighten's eyes.

"You're too fuckin' slow!" she shouted, shaking her head. She started walking back, refusing to leave her friend to these strangers.

"Hangin' with you is gonna get me killed," Kris said as she reached the group. She glanced at the big man. "Father and Mother, you're ugly." She looked at all three. "Actually, the lot of you might be the ugliest people I've ever seen here, besides this slow-ass Brighten here."

Kris was back to her "couldn't give a fuck" attitude, although Brighten was scared stiff.

"Tell us what ya want, because I was havin' lunch before ya showed up and grabbed me," Kris scolded.

"She's got a mouth on her, don't she?" the one called Verith said, chuckling.

"I'm sure you bought that lunch, huh?" the big man asked. "You little street urchin, I betcha stole it from some hard-workin' man."

"Stole it from your mother," Kris shot back. "Now what do you want?"

The older woman stepped in. "A ship came here yesterday; you see it?"

Brighten nodded. "We saw it."

"Well, *he* did," Kris told them. "He's slow as hell, but he's smart, and he's got eyes like a fuckin' hawk."

"Good." The old lady smiled. "That's what we want to talk about. The ship and this kingdom. Mainly the kingdom; do you know anything about that?"

"Sure as hell do." Kris grinned. "But it's gonna cost ya."

"Aw, hell," the big man grumbled. "We're being held up by kids who barely reach my belt buckle."

Harold and Rendal shared the same room, one lacking the furnishings Rendal was used to.

Harold was fine with the room, but he had no idea what was about to happen.

They'd been ushered into this room and questioned for a few hours. Rendal handled all the questions, not showing any stress. Even when they asked about his bracelets, he was completely confident.

"Oh, these? Just little pieces of jewelry. Personally, I don't like them, but some of the places I visit find the stones in them beautiful. Leads to better sales."

He had smiled as if to say, "Who can blame me?"

The questioning went on, but all the answers were the same: they were merchants looking to talk to the Prefect to set up favorable trading terms. No, he would not meet with anyone else. No, he was not armed. If the Prefect would not see him, then the Prefect would be withholding a steady stream of valuables at reasonable prices from his people.

"What if they don't bring you to him?" Harold asked.

Rendal lay on a cot on the other side of the room. His hands were behind his head while he stared at the ceiling.

"Oh, they will, Harold."

"I don't doubt you, sir, but why?"

Rendal didn't look over. "Because of the nine ships on the horizon. Never underestimate human greed, Harold. Not everyone holds your values. It's not power this man serves, but greed. Those ships mean money for him and for his people. He'll see me."

Harold stared at his master, hardly able to believe it. "Were you planning this? Was that one of the reasons we picked up so many ships?"

"Of course, Harold. The men on board will definitely help with my plans of militaristic conquest, but the ships help when other means are necessary."

The door to the room opened. Harold didn't look up.

"Prefect Slidell has agreed to see you, Hemmons. The accountant will remain here."

"That's fine!" Rendal hopped up. "Harold's a big boy. He can take of himself. Let's go see the Prefect."

The guard stared at Hemmons as if he had two heads, and Harold thought only a single sentence: *This city is doomed.*

Rendal followed the guard through the castle to the tower. He admired the tower and thought he would add one to

New Perth when he returned. In reality, he thought there was a lot New Perth could learn from this place.

The climb up the tower was long, but Rendal didn't mind. He had the energy of an eighteen-year-old and thought he might actually be hearing the guard above him huffing just a bit.

They reached the top of the stairs, and Rendal looked out the window to his right. He loved the view; it was simply gorgeous. The kingdom stretched as far as the eye could see.

Yes, this would make a good vacation home.

"We've arrived," the guard said stuffily.

"Oh?" Rendal asked as if he were dumb. "Is that what the door means?"

"Watch your tongue, merchant."

Rendal decided he would drop the man from this tower when he was finished with the Prefect.

The guard knocked on the door three times with a closed fist.

"Enter," the Prefect answered.

The guard pulled the large handle and stepped in.

"Your Majesty, I present the merchant from earlier: Rendal Hemmons."

"Thank you," the Prefect replied. "You may leave us."

The guard bowed slightly and turned. He looked at Rendal as he passed, and the mage grinned at him.

See you soon, he thought, knowing that the guard would feel a hint of the words but not know where they came from.

He turned to Slidell.

"They tell me you're an important man," the Prefect

told him. "That you have ten ships waiting on the ocean for us, all filled to the brim with bounty you're willing to trade. Is that true?"

He was youthful, with dark hair and a square jaw. He looked more like a politician than a mage.

"It is, your Majesty," Rendal answered. "For the right price."

"They didn't tell me you practiced magic as well," the Prefect commented. "Most likely my guards couldn't tell."

Astute, Rendal thought, unable to keep from grinning.

"I do. Much like what I've heard of Sidnie, where I come from, magic is freely practiced."

"Yes, that's true. We encourage it here, and even allow local practitioners to set up shop and teach it. Sidnie is a free place, and most magic is welcome." The Prefect moved out from behind his large desk. "It all depends on the user's intent."

"I've used no magic here, nor do I intend to, your Majesty. I only wish to grow a profitable relationship."

The Prefect wasn't a trusting man. "Then why do you keep the ships with your goods so far from our shores. Why not bring them with you?"

Rendal gave a sly smile. "And what if your intentions weren't as pure as mine, Prefect? I'd have lost all of my goods as well as my life."

The Prefect grinned back. "Come and sit with me, Rendal. Let's talk about your terms."

"Of course, your Majesty."

They made their way to the middle of the room, where two large couches sat opposite each other. Rendal waited for the Prefect, then sat down himself.

"Where are you from, Rendal?" Slidell asked.

Rendal pulled a coin from his pocket and began to flip it back and forth between his first two fingers. "Oh, you know, here and there."

The Prefect's eyes went to the coin. "Well, where do you hail from now?"

Rendal watched the man, his own eyes growing narrow. "A bit farther north than this."

The coin kept flipping. Back and forth. Back and forth.

"What kind…" the Prefect's speech slowed a bit. "What kind of terms are you looking for, Rendal? I wouldn't have agreed to see you if not for the ships outside."

Rendal started flipping the coin across four fingers.

Flip, flip, flip, flip.

Brief pause.

And then the return.

Flip, flip, flip, flip.

"If I can be honest with you, Prefect Slidell, I was thinking about a partnership between you and me."

The Prefect's eyes were growing wider, and Rendal started grinning.

"I…like…that…idea," the Prefect said extremely slowly.

It was hard to use magic when you weren't in complete control of your mind.

"You and I should talk much longer than the thirty minutes you gave me, wouldn't you agree?"

The Prefect nodded.

"Finding it hard to talk, Prefect Slidell?"

Another nod.

Rendal nodded right back. "Good. That's how we want it."

The door opened, and Harold looked up. He had no sword, no weapon at all, and would have to try brawling his way out of here if shit went south.

A guard stood in the doorway.

"The Prefect would like to see you."

Harold showed no sign of fear or excitement. He simply stood.

Internally, he thought the master was either dead or in charge of the fucking place by now.

He didn't know which. Either was possible.

Harold looked at the guard, hoping to see a tell, but got nothing.

"All right," Harold responded. "Let's go, then."

They went up the many steps in silence, Harold's senses on high alert.

They reached the door, and the guard knocked three times.

"Send him in," someone called. "Stay outside, guard."

The voice sounded sleepy, and for the first time, Harold could feel the guard's unease.

"You may enter," the guard told him.

Harold pulled the door open and stepped inside.

A young man stood ten feet in front of him. He didn't see the master anywhere.

"Please…shut the…door," the man instructed.

Harold did as he was told.

"Ah! Harold, so glad you could make it!" Rendal called. He stepped out of the corner, his eyes turning from red to their normal color. "Sorry about that, Harold. I had to make sure the guard didn't see me. We have to keep up appearances right now."

"Sir," Harold spoke, "I don't think I understand." He kept staring at the man in front of him.

"Ohhh, sorry." Rendal smiled and walked across the room. He placed his arm over the man's shoulders. "This here is Prefect Lawrence Slidell." He looked at the Prefect, who stared forward blankly. "Prefect Slidell, meet my main man Harold!"

The Prefect didn't move.

"He's so bad with manners." Rendal smiled wider and released the Prefect.

"Sir, what's happening?" Harold asked.

The mage walked to the large wooden desk, sat down in the chair, and propped his feet on the desk. "How ya like my new digs, Harold?"

Harold only swallowed.

Rendal laughed. "Lighten up! The Prefect over there is ours now. We got the run of the place, just like I said we would!"

"I don't mean to question you, sir, but how?"

"Prefect Slidell, can you come here for a second?"

Harold watched the man turn from staring at the door and walk over to the desk. He looked straight ahead blankly.

"Pick your nose, Prefect," the mage commanded.

Sure enough, the Prefect put his pointer finger in his nose and started rooting around.

"He's digging for gold!" Rendal shouted, laughing.

"How… How are you doing that?" Harold asked.

"Harold, for all the skill you've got with a sword, you

sure don't know much about persuasion. I hypnotized the bastard. All the magic in this kingdom, why would I attack them? I don't need to. I just need to control this single man and the rest of the place is mine."

Harold's eyes narrowed.

"I know, you're wondering why I didn't do that with New Perth. They know me there. Wouldn't work. Plus, I don't want to hide in the shadows there, you know? I want my face to be seen."

Harold was starting to understand.

"I've got a pretty face, Harold. You know this." The mage couldn't stop smiling.

"So, you've already taken the city…just like that?" Harold asked.

"Yes, Harold. You're seeing it now. The city is ours. I'll have to re-hypnotize this little fella every twelve hours or so, but he's going to do everything I say from now on."

Rendal stood from the chair and walked over to the zombie-like Prefect.

"We'll start slowly," he continued with a devilish grin. "Warm these people up. What's that saying? 'You can put a frog into a pot of water and slowly turn the heat up until they boil to death?' They won't realize what's happening until it's too late."

He glanced at Harold.

"That's what we're going to do here, and when Riley sees how bad it gets, she'll break. Now, go bring the rest of the ships in, then bring Mason to me." He clapped the Prefect on the back. "Welcome to the team!"

"Hear ye, hear ye! Gather 'round, everyone!"

Brighten and Kris stood at the back of the crowd, although it was growing thicker by the moment and pushing them farther back. Brighten was fine with that; he would be able to hear and see fine.

"I swear, when I get older and bigger, I'mma bust these people in the lip for thinkin' they can push me this way and that," Kris growled.

She was less content with the situation.

"By Royal Proclamation, Prefect Lawrence Slidell is creating a Royal School of Magic Training. While the Prefect is appreciative of everything that the local practitioners have done to teach magic, the Royal Proclamation hereby commands the shutting down of all individual magic teachers. This Proclamation will be posted throughout the Kingdom. Long live the Prefect!"

The crowd was silent, almost spookily so. Brighten watched and listened as people turned to each other and whispered, not understanding what exactly was happening —or why.

"William's gonna wanna hear this," Brighten said.

"For bein' so smart, you sure say the dumbest things. Looks like he's done, aye?"

Brighten nodded. The guard who'd read the proclamation was nailing the paper to a wooden pole behind him.

"Let's get back to base," Brighten whispered.

"Base, huh? That what you're callin' the shack these rabble-rousers are livin' in? They're in Shantyville, for goodness' sake." Kris smiled. "Come on. Race you!"

She took off and Brighten wanted to slug her in the

shoulder. It wasn't fair to begin with, but certainly not when she got a head start.

He bolted forward, trying to keep up but knowing it was hopeless. They wound through the streets they both knew like the backs of their hands.

It took about fifteen minutes to get from the center of town to the shanty on the edge.

Kris walked in first and Brighten followed.

"Hey, fatso," she said as she passed William.

"All that talk, little lady, but you won't pick up a sword and face me, will you?" the big man asked from his chair on the other side of the room.

"I would, but I'd simply run around in circles until you tired out and keeled over. Prolly take 'bout thirty seconds," Kris shot back.

"Enough." Lucie stepped in from the kitchen.

Brighten liked having these people here, and he thought Kris did too. He *especially* liked their cooking. This might be a shanty in the poorest part of the kingdom, but Lucie knew her way around a fire.

Even now the place smelled of roasted rabbit. Something was going on in the back, although Lucie would shoo Brighten away if he tried to get to it.

"You's right," Kris answered. "Somethin' is most definitely going on in the tower. Prefect just put out a notice that all the magic shops are to be shut down—"

"What's that mean?" William interrupted.

"If you'd shut yer trap, I could tell ya," Kris quipped. "The proclamation said the Prefect was startin' a magic school or somethin'. I don't know. What do you think, Brighten?"

Brighten had been quiet since entering. He liked the banter between William and Kris, although he didn't feel completely comfortable yet.

"The magic school don't make sense," he answered. He'd been thinking about it during their run here. "Sidnie supports as many people learnin' magic as it can. I know not everybody can, but I'd be willin' to bet a higher percentage practices magic here than anywhere else because of how strong it's supported. Shuttin' down the magic shops and then creatin' a school? That goes against everything."

Kris was nodding along.

"Tell us more, Brighten," Lucie prodded.

She could tell he'd been thinking.

"Could be what ya said. Could be those two men got control over the Prefect," he answered.

"Ain't none of that true, Brighten," Kris interjected. "I done told ya. These people lyin', and the only reason I'm stickin' around is because this lady can *cook*."

He knew she was joking.

They both were starting to believe.

Lucie had broken down the story for them last night. Some mage from miles and miles away had been kidnapping people from Sidnie for years and holding them captive while he sucked their magic from them.

It sounded crazy.

"Sure does," Kris had said.

Yet there *had* been kidnappings. Everybody knew about them. They were sporadic, but the kingdom would wake up one morning, and ten or twenty people would simply be missing.

It'd been happening for years.

There wasn't any official doctrine on it from the Prefect, but the townspeople knew it. Everyone, and Brighten meant *everyone*, knew of someone who'd simply gone missing.

"Aye." William glanced at Kris. "I hope you get taken next, sure 'nuff."

"Would you two please focus?" Lucie asked. "You two are at least as bad as Riley when she's around. Now, this makes sense, if ya think about it. He's been stealing magic forever from this place, but if he has control over it, why not just bring them all right to him?"

"Maybe, maybe not," Erin said.

Brighten thought the woman was beautiful, and he knew William did too. Every single time she spoke, the big man straightened up a bit. Brighten didn't think William even noticed; it was simply automatic.

Lucie turned to the redhaired beauty. "Go on."

"By all means," William added.

Kris rolled her eyes but said nothing, noticing that Brighten did too.

"Well, maybe he doesn't *need* to make himself more powerful—not if he can get the magic folks here to simply serve him. Wouldn't that be easier? Use a lot less energy?"

"That's really smart." William nodded.

"Oh, give it a rest." Kris looked like she might roll her eyes so hard, they'd fall out of her head.

"The Prefect is calling for everyone who can use magic? There's no other requirement?" Lucie asked.

"That's what the Proclamation said," Brighten answered.

Lucie nodded, then looked at the ground. "It's too early to tell what he's going to do. The Prefect remains in that tower, right?"

"I've been askin' 'round," Kris answered. "The Prefect has his meetings up there and makes decisions from up there, but most people like him. Even those from our side of town, because he makes a point of showin' his face outside of the tower. He ain't done that since the ships showed up, though. He's stayed locked up at the top."

"And no one has seen the two men who went up?"

Kris shook her head.

"The other ships came in. They're at the docks now," Brighten volunteered.

"Has anyone gotten off?" William asked.

Brighten shook his head. "Not that I've seen. No one has gone on either."

"*That* is interesting. You'd think they'd at least be checked out," Erin said.

"Don't agree with her, William," Kris got out before anyone else could talk, and grinned.

William's face turned red.

Lucie ignored Kris. "The Prefect is under Rendal's control. I suppose he could have put a necklace on him, but that would be too obvious. He must be using some other method."

"Like what?" William asked.

"I'm not sure, but Erin is right. They'd be searchin' those ships if the Prefect ordered them to come to the docks." Lucie looked at Brighten and Kris. "How close can you two get to that tower?"

Kris grinned. "Depends on whatcha have to offer."

Brighten shook his head. "No. No, Kris. We ain't doin' that again. We're not goin' near that tower. I don't care what they have, and I don't care what you say. We're not goin'."

"He's a wimp." Kris grinned, ignoring Brighten's protests. "We can get all the way to the top of the tower. We did it before on a dare—"

"We almost died!" Brighten shouted.

"But did we?" Kris whipped around to him, still grinning. "Nope. We lived." She looked back at Lucie. "We can get up there and see what's goin' on, but it's gonna cost ya, lady, and more than the rabbit stew you're makin'. What can ya offer?"

William stood. "I could offer not to pummel you until you're nothing but a puddle."

"Oh, please, fatso." Kris laughed, taking none of it seriously—as she did her entire life. "You'd have to catch me first. Now, seriously. You want to know what's happening, you're gonna have to cough up something. We'll be able to move 'round the whole castle and pick up a ton of information."

Verith spoke from the other side of the shanty. "If you help us and we live, I can guarantee you that you'll never have to steal bread from the market again. You'll have enough wealth to live wherever you want in luxury."

"How can he guarantee that, Kris?" Brighten stressed.

"Because I'm the top general in New Perth, and our Assistant Prefect was kidnapped and is on those ships. If you help us, our Prefect will reward you handsomely."

Kris' eyes narrowed as she considered Verith's offer.

"You *know* it's dangerous, Kris. It's not worth it."

Kris quit staring and smiled again. "I believe 'em, and you don't have to come, Brighten, but you ain't gonna get none of my gold if you stay here."

Kris spat on her hand and extended it to Verith. "Shake on it. Make it official."

The general stared at the dirty hand for a second, then shrugged. "When in Sidnie, I suppose." He spat on his own hand and shook the girl's.

"All right, we'll be back in a couple of days. Try not to get yourselves killed." Kris turned to Brighten. "Come on, wuss. I don't want all this gold to myself."

She grabbed Brighten firmly and yanked him out of the shanty.

CHAPTER TWELVE

"Who told you how to find us?"

Riley stood inside the room—the *queen's* room, although Riley wasn't sure exactly what she was queen *of*.

"The man outside the door," Riley answered. "His name is Worth."

The woman in front of her had long blonde hair and the same color gray eyes as the people Riley had already met. She was pretty, although not beautiful like Erin.

She sat on a couch with her arms spread across the back.

"What did he say to you?" she asked.

The queen was just as serious as the other strangers had been.

"Well..." Riley thought for a second. "Worth speaks a bit differently from other people. He said your people needed big magic. He said that was the only way you'd come out."

"Big magic? That's what he called it?" the queen asked.

Riley nodded.

"And you're the one who made the big magic?"

Again, she nodded.

"What else did he say?" The queen was clearly judging Riley before having even properly introduced herself.

"Not a lot. He calls you underground people."

The queen nodded. "Sit down." She gestured toward a chair facing her.

Riley joined the queen.

"My name is Alexandra. Your friend Worth is right. We do look for 'big magic,' and it seems you have that. Who are you?"

Riley didn't sense danger here and started to let her guard down some.

"I'm the Right Hand for New Perth. I serve the Assistant Prefect. I have some questions myself," Riley answered.

"In due time. First, tell me why you and your friend Worth were looking for us?"

Riley sighed, chuckled, and looked at her feet. "That's a long story."

"Give me the short version. There will be time for the long one later."

Riley nodded. "Basically, people keep telling me I have a lot of magic potential, but I haven't been able to unlock it. The only time I can do anything with it is when I or someone I love is in real danger of dying. Other than that, it's locked away from me."

"I see." Alexandria nodded. "And your friend Worth…is he from the Badlands?"

"Yes."

"He's the one who told you to come to us?" the queen asked.

Riley looked at her. "He said you could train me."

The queen still showed no emotion. "Now ask your questions."

"Well, first, how the hell were those raiders up there invisible?"

Riley saw the first hint of a grin at the corner of the queen's lips. "A little trick is all. It's a pretty sophisticated piece of technology, but they aren't actually invisible. They just cloak themselves. Did you see stone packs on their belts?"

Riley nodded.

"Those power the cloaking devices, which basically mimic whatever is around them. It allows them to look like the sand and sky. They hope they run across people traveling like you were. You smelled the burning?"

"It was awful," Riley answered.

"That's from the technology. It gives them away to those who know the smell." Alexandria crossed one leg over the other. "What else?"

"What is this place?" Riley asked.

"They called it a fallout shelter, but it was only for the upper echelon of people. It was supposed to protect them from the technology they created to kill everyone." Finally, the queen did give an ironic little smile. "I don't think anyone made it, though, because when we found it, it was empty."

"And who *are* you?" Riley finally asked. "Underground people? The Chosen? What's all of it mean?"

"Ah, we get to the heart of the matter." Alexandra

nodded to the door behind Riley. "Your friend Worth… why is he in the Badlands?"

"Many in his clan are mutants. They were chased out of other cities from what I understand," Riley answered.

"We were chased out too." Alexandra had a knowing look in her eyes. "My mother and my father, although for different reasons. They were waiting for a savior, but no one wanted to hear it. They were waiting for someone who would arrive with enough power to move the world forward again."

"Forward?" Riley's eyes narrowed.

"Yes. The green stones give us power and we have some bare technology, but nothing like the legends speak of. My parents were 'futurists,' but what that really meant was they wanted to go *back* in time. They wanted to bring real technology to the world again. Combine that with magic, and the potential for humanity would be unlimited." The woman's eyes grew distant as she spoke.

"Your parents were chased out of different kingdoms?" Riley felt for the woman.

"Yes. Largely because they truly believed that someone would come who could move us into the future, or rather, into our past." The queen's eyes focused again. "That was why your friend Worth thought we would train you. Because if you're powerful enough, perhaps we'll think you are that person."

"Worth's a tricky bastard." Riley grinned for a moment, then let it fade. "But I need to be honest with you. I'm no savior. I'm not bringing anyone into the future. I'm trying to save the man I serve and the city I love—that's it."

The queen gave a gracious smile. "Do you know how

many years we've looked for magic like you showed up there?"

"That? All I did was lift some people." Riley was confused. She'd done more against Rendal.

"The Chosen are very sensitive to magic use. My parents trained us how to be. You only lifted those people, true, but there was an undercurrent of power that none of us have felt before. That was why Thomas went aboveground to see. We weren't sure what was happening." The queen stood and walked closer to the door.

Riley turned around and watched.

"My parents never said that the savior would know they were the savior, only that they needed to manifest a certain threshold of magic. If they had it, then they could do what was needed."

Riley honestly didn't know how to respond. She wasn't a savior, and she wasn't going to be that for these people. She needed to know how to use magic so she could go save Mason.

"You have that threshold," the queen said. "You want to learn how to use your magic. That's why you've come?"

Riley nodded. "Yes."

"Then we'll teach you. We'll make sure that no parts of your power are blocked from you."

Riley stood. "I need you to understand that I will appreciate you doing that for me, but I won't serve you. I won't be a leader here. That's not what my life is about."

Alexandra smiled. "I understand you say that now, and that's fine. We don't always pick our paths in this world, though. Sometimes they pick us. Let's see if we can't get your magic out of you, and then we'll see about saving the world, okay?"

Riley swallowed. She didn't know what she was agreeing to, but she knew Mason and New Perth needed her.

But Riley had told the woman the truth. She hadn't lied.

Riley grinned. "Yeah. Let's learn some magic."

CHAPTER THIRTEEN

"Watch, Harold. Watch." Rendal turned to Slidell. "Stand on one leg."

Slidell dutifully did as he was told.

Rendal started laughing.

"Go on, you try." Rendal grinned at Harold. "I've hypnotized him to listen to you too so that we can both have fun."

Harold looked at the Prefect, clearly not wanting anything to do with this dazed man.

"Go on," Rendal urged.

"Tap the top of your head," Rendal told him.

"No, no. You have to say his name. He's used to *me* talking to him, not you."

Rendal thought this hilarious.

"Slidell," Harold started, "tap your head."

The man's hand moved to his scalp and started lightly patting it while still standing on one leg.

"He'll do it forever!" Rendal exclaimed. "Well, until the hypnosis wears off."

"How long is that?"

"Oh, it's getting stronger, which means it'll last longer. The more I use it on him, the deeper he goes under."

"Can he even talk anymore?" Harold asked.

Rendal nodded. "Yes, but it's more sluggish. That's one of the problems. His guards aren't completely happy."

"But they're still obeying him?" Harold stared at the Prefect, who was still following both of their commands.

"For now. We may need a more elegant solution sooner or later, but that's down the road yet." Rendal turned away from the foolish-looking Prefect. "You've been working with the guards, correct? How is the magic school coming?"

"There's been some unrest in the streets. The people who teach magic aren't happy with the proclamation," Harold answered.

Rendal waved his hand as if shooing away the news. "Let them cry to someone else, you know, Harold? We men of substance have more important things to worry about." He smiled. "I've been working on a curriculum while you've been busy setting everything up."

"A curriculum?" Harold asked.

Rendal nodded. He'd actually put a good bit of time into it. Things were looking much, much better than he'd originally thought possible. He was going to have a school to train mages, and all of them would end up doing his bidding. "I'd like the most advanced students in one class, then a second tier, and then a third, you understand?"

"I can do that, sir."

Harold looked at Mason and Rendal followed his gaze. "How are ya, Mason?" Rendal asked.

"I'd speak, but I'm not dumb, Rendal. You'll throw me

back in one of those cages if I talk too much, so I'll say whatever you want. How do you want me to be?"

Rendal laughed. "See, Harold? Another form of hypnotism! *He'll* do whatever I want, too!"

Rendal was genuinely in good spirits—except for one thing. He turned to Harold, his smile fading. He forgot about Mason. "Riley. Have you heard anything about her? Is she here?"

"No, sir," Harold responded. "So far there's been no sightings. We're still looking, though."

Riley's coming here was important. He needed her to see what he was doing, but maybe it was better that she wasn't here yet. The longer it took her, the more pain the city would suffer.

"Keep your eyes out," Rendal instructed. "I want to have class this evening. Get the first group ready—the most advanced."

"Yes, sir. Right away."

Harold left the room, glancing at the Prefect as he did. The man was still standing on one foot and patting his head.

"Oh, stop, Slidell," Rendal commanded.

"That's the best, ain't it?" Kris asked.

Brighten nodded. About a hundred kids stood in rows inside the town square. Brighten recognized a couple of them, but not a lot. Those kids didn't mix with the homeless like him.

He only knew the few because they'd become easy marks for him and Kris.

"Why are they lining all them up?" she wondered aloud. "You think that's part of the school?"

"S'gotta be," Brighten answered.

Kris looked at him with a grin on her face. "You want to join 'em?"

"Fuck, no!" Brighten shouted. "Are you outta your damn mind? Can't neither of us use magic. We'd be caught soon as we got into the classroom. Probably as soon as we try to get in those lines."

"Wellllll," Kris drew out the word as she looked toward the group, "that's *partly* true. I don't know any magic, but you got a little bit in you, doncha?"

Brighten shook his head hard. "*No.*"

"You just gonna sit here and lie to me like that, Brighten? We both know you been known to use a little magic trickery when we're stealin' from folks."

Brighten looked down at his feet. It was nothing. Just suggestions his mind made to get a mark to look a little more this way or that.

"And them people back in the shanty," Kris continued. "As much shit as I give 'em, they seem decent enough, and they're right. Something *is* goin' on here. Something's *been* goin' on with all those people kidnapped over the years. You're just gonna slow me down getting to the top of that tower, but you *can* get into that group and that class."

"I don't want to," Brighten told her.

"Yeah, yeah. You don't never wanna do nothin'. Don't even wanna steal, but I make ya do that." Kris looked at him, taking a step closer. "We need to know what's goin' on in there because them people at the shanty need to know."

Brighten sighed. "You're gonna end up gettin' me killed, Kris."

She laughed. "You been sayin' that for years. Still alive, aincha? And look, we're gonna be rich if you just keep listenin' to me. Go on and get in there."

A guard walked out from the large building in front of the group of kids.

"This everybody?" he shouted.

Kris shoved him. "Go!"

Brighten shook his head as he rushed forward. He knew if he didn't follow her directions, he was just asking for an earful later.

He hustled across the open pavilion, leaving his friend behind. He was afraid, but then, he was always afraid. It was just a part of what made Brighten, and he usually didn't let it stop him, despite his protests.

"You're late!" the guard shouted.

That's odd, Brighten thought. The guards usually weren't super-dicks.

"Very sorry, sir. Won't happen again." Brighten drew up behind the last row of kids.

"Make sure it doesn't!" the guard yelled. "This everybody?"

Brighten looked him over. He didn't know *all* the guards, but he didn't think he'd ever seen this one. Brighten knew the *important* ones, the ones who could get you locked up for stealin' a piece of cheese just by lookin' atcha.

This man wasn't one of those, but why would they put someone unimportant over this inaugural class?

"My name is Belarus, you snot-nosed brats, and you'll be listenin' to me whenever you're *not* in class. You understand?"

A lot of nods and a lot of verbal affirmations. Brighten just watched.

"Right now, you're gonna be taken before the bos—the *headmaster.*"

Brighten heard that mix-up clearly. Belarus had started to call the man his boss, then corrected himself.

"You get into a single file line and follow me, then you'll meet Headmaster Hemmons."

Headmaster Hemmons? Brighten had never heard the name in his life. If anyone were to teach this type of class, it would be Prefect Slidell.

Lucie was right. Something was definitely wrong here.

Kris *was* worried, but she didn't do that shit in front of Brighten. That poor boy might lose his mind if she said a word about what worried her.

She never felt anxiety about Brighten, though. She'd known him her whole life, and they'd been running the streets together since they were old enough to run 'em. He wasn't as athletic as her, but his senses were out of this world, and he was the smartest person Kris had ever met.

What she worried about right now was getting up in that tower.

Of course, she would never worry as much as Brighten.

She watched the group of kids walk into the new "Royal School of Magic Training." What a dumb fuckin' name that was. They needed something more exciting—the Mage Academy, maybe.

Yeah, that would work.

Kris waited until they'd left and then stepped out from the shadows. The sun was going down, and the young thief needed to slip into the Prefect's castle. Shift change was comin' up for the guards, so she sped across the pavilion.

The castle was close to this newly repurposed magic building, but she wasn't slippin' in through the front.

She stuck to the growing shadows, and she moved quickly over the cobblestones. Kris was an excellent thief, maybe the best in the whole homeless population.

Connor would disagree, she told herself.

Then, *Fuck Connor.*

She hoped she'd never have to see him again.

The castle was large and had a tall concrete fence around it. At the front were metal gates and a sentry.

Kris wasn't heading anywhere near that, though.

She made her way around the circular fence, staying in the shadows of the buildings a bit farther away.

Sentries were placed every hundred feet, but that was mainly for show. No one had ever attacked the castle or tried to gain unauthorized entrance—except for Kris.

Fuckin' Connor never tried, she thought with some satisfaction. *Claims he's the best thief in Sidnie, but ain't never tried to get into the tower.*

It was a going bet among the homeless kids—who was fast witted and athletic enough to make it up to the top of the tower?

Kris and Brighten had done it once.

Connor had never even tried and then attempted to tell everyone else that Kris was lyin' about it.

Quit thinkin' about him, she told herself as she slowed down. *You got stuff here to worry about now.*

So she did. The shift change was occurring, and she watched as the new sentry took the day shift guard's spot. She waited until the day shift guard had walked far enough away, then stepped out of the shadows.

The sentry stared straight ahead as if he didn't hear or see her.

She walked right up to him, and still the sentry didn't so much as glance down. He was a foot taller than her.

"You look idiotic in that hat," Kris said loudly.

The sentry didn't look down.

"I mean, really. You look like a damned moron, Billy."

"Hush your mouth," Billy whispered harshly.

Kris smiled. "Oh, so you *can* see me. For a second there, I was thinkin' I ain't exist."

"What do you want?"

"Ya gotta let me in." Kris grinned wildly.

The sentry broke countenance and looked down at her. "Fuck, no. No way. I did that once for your little fuckin' game with them kids, but I ain't doin' it again. I could get put in the stocks if I get caught."

"Didja get caught last time?" Riley asked.

"That's not the point."

"It's the only point I see. Now, come on, quit playin' around. I need to make some moves while the castle is at dinner. You know it's easier right now."

The sentry looked up as if he had heard nothing, staring forward again.

"Billllllly," Kris whined. "I won't getcha caught. What the hell would Mom say if she was alive? Probably somethin' along the lines of, 'You need to help your *little sister.*'"

Billy didn't look down. "If she were alive, she'd tell me to do everything I could to keep this job and to not do *anything* you ask me to. Especially not dumb pranks."

"All right, all right, I hear ya. But this isn't a prank. Last time it was. This time, I need to get in because somethin' bad is goin' on."

Billy looked down. "How do you know?"

That told Kris all she needed to know. He'd noticed too.

"It's all over the damn city. The guards are meaner, not to mention that fuckin' *magic* school they got. Shuttin' down all the normal teachers."

Billy's eyes narrowed. "What business do you got goin' up there? Even if things aren't right, what are you gonna do about it?"

"Billy, just trust me. I'm your damn sister. There are other people involved. Foreigners, not from here. They're the ones asked me to come. I *need* your help."

Billy looked left and right, checking his surroundings. The other sentries weren't visible, given the fence's curvature.

Kris dropped all pretense of joking. "I'm serious. This is important. It ain't no bet with the kids."

"Damn it, Kris." Billy sighed. "I swear, you're gonna feel guilty if I get in trouble for this. They'll see us both hanged."

"Well, then I won't have to feel guilty for long, will I?" Her grin returned.

Night had arrived, and the entire area was darker.

Billy turned around and faced the fence. It was too high to jump over, but that wasn't their plan.

He took a step back. "Did you tell any of your dirty-ass friends about this?"

"Of course not. I'm not *evil*. I'm just a bitch." She winked at him.

He sighed again and knelt, then pulled a ring of keys from his belt and moved the grass around in front of him for a moment. Finding what he wanted, he stuck the key in and twisted.

"Help me, nimwit," he grumbled.

Kris got down on her knees and felt for the secret door with her hands. All the sentries stood guard over one, and only their keys would open them. It was, truth be told, silly to even have them; no one was going to try to break into the damn castle.

At least, that was what Kris *had* thought.

Now she knew that wasn't the case.

They lifted the door, the dirt and grass ripping apart at its edges. Billy would have to fix it later.

He stood up, still holding the door.

"Thanks, bro." Kris smiled at him. "I owe ya one."

"You're damn right ya do. First, take this." He handed her a key. "You'll need it to open the other side, just like last time. Get it back to me tomorrow, and don't *ever* ask me to do this again."

"If I don't tell ya no promises, I can't ever be a liar." Smiling, Kris dropped into the blackness below.

She fell only about seven feet, and she landed without any pain. Kris was light and athletic, so a short drop didn't matter.

"Touch the wall panel for a few seconds," her brother whispered into the hole.

"I know!" she shouted back. What did he think she was, an idiot who couldn't remember six months ago?

She touched her hand to the stone on the right and waited a bit. It started glowing green, then lights fluttered on down the hallway.

"Thanks again!"

The door slammed shut above, and she took off. The hallway wasn't long, but the quicker she got out of it, the less likely Billy was to get caught.

He'd worked his ass off for that job, and it was something no kid from the streets should ever get. He said five years ago he was done stealin', done lootin', and was turning straight no matter what it took.

And now he was workin' as a sentry for the damned Prefect. Kris was proud of him.

She reached the end of the tunnel and thoughts of her brother dissipated.

Metal bars were screwed into the wall, creating a ladder.

Kris climbed it rapidly and used her brother's key to open the door.

I love that sonofabitch, she thought.

She climbed through the hole and then was inside the castle walls, then turned to her left and looked at the tower.

The lights were on inside, shining brightly into the

night sky.

"Yeah, something's goin' on up there," Kris whispered.

She got her bearings by looking around the large yard in front of her. This was when she needed Brighten's damned sharp eyes. He'd have been able to pick out any guards before they were even out of the hole.

Kris didn't see any, so she hurried across the yard. The large trees planted there helped shield her from anyone who might be looking.

She could see into the Royal Dining Room, servants coming and going and people sitting at a large table.

Which was where Kris wanted them.

She skipped the rest of the way across the lawn and flattened herself against the building.

"Yeah, fuck 'em."

The words came from Kris' left, just beyond the building's curve.

"Something ain't right about 'em," another voice said. "It ain't just that they *think* they're in charge. They actually *are* in charge now, and I don't know how the Prefect decided that."

"Ha! Prefect. More like puppet. That merchant must have bought him off with a pretty hefty bribe," the first voice growled.

Kris needed to get into the building, but she wanted to hear more.

She slowly crept around the side of the building, ducking to avoid the windows.

"What can ya offer a Prefect? What kinda price would make him trade his kingdom?" the second guard asked.

"I don't know, but have you seen 'im?"

"The Prefect?"

"Yeah," the first guard answered. "I saw 'im last night before I came out here to smoke. Saw him shuffling to that dining room in there. That merchant has him drugged or something. He looks half-asleep, eyes barely open."

"You think that's it?" the second guard asked.

"I don't know what it is, but *something* is different. His damned advisors need to do their jobs and see what the hell is goin' on."

Kris moved no farther; if she did, she'd be right in front of them. She pressed herself against the building, trying to disappear as best she could.

"Hard for them to say anything when he's holed up in that tower all day," the second guard continued.

"Then they need to grab 'im when he comes down to dinner. Something's gotta be done before this goes too far."

Kris turned away from them. That was all she needed to hear. The Prefect would come down to dinner, which would probably last an hour or an hour and a half at most.

She had to move if she wanted to get up there.

Kris went the opposite direction of the guards, the smell of their cigarettes fading as she rushed away.

She slipped in a side door. The dining room was on the south side of the building, the tower on the north.

It didn't matter how fast Kris was—there were simply too many people in this damned place for her to run straight for the tower. She'd be seen and brought down before she made it another hundred feet. Getting this far inside was unheard of.

She needed different clothes.

Last time she and Brighten had found them in the kitchen, and that was where she headed now.

She didn't run as she had outside—that would be entirely too obvious. Instead, she walked, keeping her head down and doing her best imitation of a servant.

Her memory might not be as great as Brighten's, but she remembered how to get to the kitchen.

It only took her a minute or two to get to the tall doors.

"Who're you?"

A fat man was standing right in front of Kris.

"New help," she answered.

"Ain't order no new help." The man's bristling mustache hung over his upper lip.

"Didja talk to Brad?" Kris asked. She had no clue where this was going, but she'd been in more jams like this than she could count.

Confuse the marks—that was her and Brighten's motto.

"Brad?" the fat man asked.

"Yeah, Brad. He came out yesterday askin' for help."

The fat man's eyebrows raised. He was at least a foot taller than Kris. "Who the hell is Brad?"

"I don't know. Said he works for you."

"For *me*?" the fat man asked.

"Yeah, said he and Cheryl were lookin' for more folks to work the kitchen." Kris would introduce as many names as possible to confuse this fat bastard. If she didn't, she was goin' to the stocks.

"Cheryl? Girl, what are you talkin' 'bout? You ain't even dressed for kitchen work, and I don't know no Brad and Cheryl." The fat man was growing pissed.

And that wasn't good.

"Well, let's go look for 'em. Brad said he works nights."

The fat man turned to the kitchen staff, a whole host of women and men shuffling to and fro with pots and pans.

"Listen up!" he shouted. "Anyone know any damn Brad that works a night shift?"

The staff stopped and stared at their boss.

"Welp, this isn't the way I wanted it to go," Kris whispered to herself. "Fuck it."

She rushed forward, going low, and grabbed the fat man's left foot. She pulled as she ran to her right, and his legs slid out from under him. He landed with a loud crash, pans raining down on top of him.

"*HEY!*" someone shouted, but Kris hardly heard them.

She was past them, moving as easily here as she had on the cobblestones outside.

All of 'em were marks, and right now she had to steal a single thing and then get lost.

Kris rushed to her right as the group finally started to move. She glanced at the fat man, who kept slipping as he tried to regain his feet.

Kris wanted to get to the back of the kitchen, but the damn problem was, she'd have to get to the front right after.

Focus on the item, not the getaway, Brighten always said. *You focus on the getaway, you'll never get the item.*

She rounded a large sink and saw what she wanted— the hanging aprons and what looked to be a chef suit.

"*GET HER!*"

Kris reached the hooks, and, hardly slowing, grabbed both items.

She turned around—

"Aye, girlie, you done fucked up now." The fat man blocked the front door.

"Did you find Brad?" she asked.

"Brad? You must think me an idiot." More people were coming behind him now, creating a barrier for her. "Ain't no Brad, and you just stole from the Prefect right there."

"With what?" Kris asked. "What'd I steal?"

She walked slowly forward, gaining ground. She knew the marks wouldn't consider her a threat because of how small she was in comparison to the fat man.

"That apron right there in yer hand. Same with the clothes."

"This stuff? Naw, Brad told me to grab 'em."

"*THERE AIN'T NO FUCKIN' BRAD!*" the fat man screamed, his face growing red.

Kris couldn't help but smile.

She was five feet from him and needed just a couple more to make the plan work.

Brighten would be proud, all this quick plannin'.

"Brad?" Kris asked, pretending to look over the man's shoulders as she kept stepping forward. "Brad, where the hell are you? Quit playin' games here! You'll get in me serious trouble!"

"Oh, it's too late, girlie—"

The fat man wanted to say something else, but Kris didn't give him time.

His legs were spread just wide enough; she launched forward feet first, sliding through them and grabbing his ankles once more.

Her weight pulled them out from under him a second time, and he hit the floor with a loud *smack*.

"AHH!" he shouted, but it was gargled, blood probably pouring from his nose.

Kris didn't have time to look, though. She ducked and shot into the crowd before her. She'd done this shit for years, creating a distraction and then simply running out.

She pulled at people's aprons and belts and feet. Some tripped, some only yelled, but the confusion was growing.

Kris reached the edge of the crowd, bursting through. Only the ones in the back saw her rushing away.

"There she is!"

But it was too late for the crowd. Kris already had the items, and these marks weren't gonna catch her.

This is harder than last time, she thought as she rounded a corner, looking for a closet to hide in for a second.

She grinned and thought sarcastically, *No worries, though. All I gotta do is climb to the top of the Prefect's tower. Should be a cinch.*

Kris slipped into a closet. There were noises coming from the kitchen, but those idiots weren't going to find her. They weren't even going to raise a stink, because fat man wasn't gonna want the whole castle knowing a teenager had broken his nose.

She closed the door, a wide smile on her face. Brighten would be pissin' his pants right now, but she loved this shit.

Brigthen *was* nearly pissin' his pants, metaphorically speaking.

He didn't know how he'd let Kris talk him into this, but it wasn't going to end well.

The group of kids—the *class*, as Brighten was coming to think of it—had entered a capacious auditorium.

"Now, y'all sit your asses down in them chairs and wait until the headmaster gets here. I don't want no questions, and no fightin'. Just keep quiet, ya understand?"

Brighten was confused for a second, not understanding the direction to keep quiet and then being asked a question. After a moment, he came to the conclusion that Belarus was not a smart man.

He smiled at that.

"What's your name?" the boy next to Brighten asked.

"Jenkins," Brighten replied without hesitation. He hadn't given his real name to a stranger in years.

"How far along are you with magic?"

Oh, help me, Father, he thought, almost physically cringing at the question.

"Far enough to be here." He didn't hang out with these kids, and he didn't know how to act around them.

But the answer seemed to suffice. "I'm Lionel, and I can tell ya one thing—that guy Belarus is a damn ass."

Brighten smiled. They could definitely agree on *that*.

"I don't know who he thinks he is, but he looks like he fell off the ugly tree and hit every damn branch on the way down, ya know what I mean?"

Brighten nodded. "It was a tall tree, too."

Lionel chuckled. "That's a good one. Look at his hand, man. All bandaged up but acting like he can kick our ass. Probably got beat up by a girl."

"Nah, probably just broke it wiping his ass."

"Ha!" Lionel actually laughed. "You're funny. I haven't seen you around. Where you been training at?"

The good thing about stealin' for a livin'? You understood every part of the city. Every nook and cranny. Every *magic shop*.

He just had to hope this kid didn't train at the same one.

"Chester's," Brighten answered.

"Ah, I went there when I was younger. A good chap, Chester. Just sucks that all these guys are losin' their businesses, and here we are ushered into some class we don't know nothin' about."

Brighten had never *disliked* the kids from the middle and upper classes. He never trusted them, though. This kid, however, seemed to be…*nervous*, just like Brighten.

You use *marks, you don't befriend them.* He could hear himself saying that to Kris, and quickly shut down any feelings of kindness.

"There he is," Lionel stated

Brighten saw him—a tall man, older but not elderly.

Belarus gave him a wide berth and clearly showed deference.

"You ever seen this guy?" Lionel asked.

Brighten shook his head. "No, never."

"Me either. He hasn't been in any magic shops around here. I've been to them all over the years." Lionel didn't trust this headmaster, and Brighten couldn't help but identify with that.

He didn't trust the man either.

"Welcome," the stranger started. "My name is Rendal Hemmons, and I'm the headmaster of the Prefect's new school. It's an honor to be here, and I'm hoping that very soon I get to work with all of you on a personal level."

"What are those?" Brighten whispered, unable to help himself.

"What?" Lionel asked.

"The bracelets on his arms. What are those?"

Lionel was quiet for a moment, clearly having not seen them. "I…I don't know. Never seen anything like them."

The headmaster's eyes caught Brighten's and held them for a second. "You all are supposed to be the best of the best, and that's why the Prefect summoned you first. You're going to become the greatest mages this kingdom has ever seen."

"Why aren't we allowed to train with our old teachers?" someone shouted from the front.

The headmaster turned his head to the boy and smiled. "You liked your old teacher, huh?"

"Yeah. He was really good," the kid answered, clearly not feeling threatened.

"You want to go back to him?" the headmaster asked.

"Yeah. I don't know why I'm here."

Rendal nodded. "Sure, then, head on back. We won't make you stay."

"What about the proclamation?" the kid asked. "Ralph already shut down his damn shop."

Rendal chuckled and looked at Belarus, who was standing just off stage. "His *damn* shop. Do you hear that, Belarus?"

"I did, bos—*headmaster*. Despicable."

The kid was more nervous now than he had been moments before.

Rendal turned back to the kid. "Well, that's right. The

shop has shut down. I hadn't thought of that… What's your name again?"

"Sal," the kid answered.

"I hadn't thought of that, *Sal*," the headmaster said. "But you're right, the shops are all closed. Thanks to our glorious Prefect, we now have a school that focuses on creating the greatest mages in the world instead of a bunch of tiny schools teaching their own kinds of magic. We have an academy that's going to make you warrior mages."

"*Warrior* mages?" Brighten whispered, turning to Lionel. "You ever heard of such a thing?"

Lionel shook his head. "No. Why would Sidnie need warrior mages? We've never been to *war*."

"Sal," the headmaster continued, "since you don't want to be here, you don't *have* to be. Belarus, please show this student to the door."

"Be my pleasure." Belarus stepped forward.

"No, no. I didn't mean that. I want to be here. I just… I just—" The kid couldn't think of what he was "just" trying to say.

Belarus hopped off the platform and walked to the front row. He grabbed the kid with his good hand, lifting him up by the back of his collar.

"You look like a rich boy," the headmaster observed. He glanced at Belarus. "If his parents try to raise a fuss, send them directly to me. He's out, and he's not coming back."

"Yes, headmaster. Understood." Belarus grinned as he spoke.

Rendal looked at the kid once more. "We'll see how you like going through life knowing no more magic than what you know right now. How's that sound?"

The kid was blubbering. Begging to be allowed to stay.

"This is brutal," Lionel whispered.

Both of them understood what was happening, the same as the kid down there did. He'd spoken up, saying he didn't want to be here, and now he wouldn't be.

Without anyone teaching magic in the kingdom, his skills might never improve. For all intents and purposes, his magic might be as good as it was ever going to be.

That sentence sent Brighten's mind down other paths. Only the people in this place would learn magic, and only at the hands of this man. Magic had been free for all who could use it for so long in Sidnie…

"But that ain't the case any longer," he thought aloud.

"Huh?" Lionel asked.

"Nothing. We better shut up before we're thrown out next."

"You're smarter than ya look, Jenkins." Lionel actually appeared frightened.

But then so did the rest of the kids in the auditorium as they listened to Sal's cries echo off the ceiling. They were all realizing just how much Sidnie had changed in a matter of days.

Kris looked like a teenage chef, although the clothes were too baggy. She hadn't heard anyone running down the halls looking for her while she changed. She imagined the kitchen staff thought she was some homeless kid playing a prank.

If they reported the break-in the guards would get in trouble, then the guards might make kitchen life hell.

Kris was just glad they weren't coming for her.

Now to get to the top of the tower.

The castle was large, and although a lot of people worked in it, there were still many empty hallways. Kris slipped down them, hardly making any noise.

The apron and chef's outfit were insurance.

It took her five minutes at a fast jog to reach the base of the tower. There were two entrances to it—the tower stood high above the castle, but at its base, there was an entrance both inside and out.

Kris reached the massive room that held the base of the tower. A guard stood on either side of the door, which was closed.

She peered around the corner at them, but they were beyond lackadaisical, like the guards outside.

They weren't sitting down, but they were leaning against the concrete blocks behind them.

"We're gonna get replaced," the shorter one said. "Sure as my fuckin' name's Sam, we're gonna get replaced."

"Yer name ain't Sam," the taller one responded with a slight grin.

"Just testin' ya, but what I say still stands. We're gonna get fired, and most likely sooner rather than later."

"Who's gonna replace us?" the taller one asked. "This job sucks donkey balls, and you know it. Ya stand here guardin' this tower as if someone's gonna try to sack it, and ya do it for twelve damned hours." He shook his head. "Who else is gonna come in here and do this?"

"I know you heard the rumors," the short one

responded. "About those men on the ships. The ones wearin' the necklaces. They're the ones about to take our places."

"I hear them rumors, but I ain't seen none of 'em. Just a bunch of scared housewives gossipin' if you ask me," the second one grumbled.

Okay, enough. Get on with it, Kris thought.

What's your plan? Brighten's voice challenged.

She didn't really have one, and that was the fuckin' problem. Last time she and Brighten had worked together to distract the guards, but now it was just her.

To hell with it, she thought. She never planned much anyway. Why start now?

She stepped out from behind the doorway and entered the circular room.

"Hiya, fellas. Been summoned upstairs." Kris grinned as if she had every right in the world to be there.

"From the kitchen?" the short guard asked.

"You're a bright one," Kris shot back. "What gave it away? The apron, or the chef's uniform?"

"Watch it, soup girl," the tall one snapped, "or you'll be the mystery meat tomorrow."

"I'm just playin', gents. The Prefect asked me to check on his guests' food upstairs, so I gotta get up there for a few minutes." Kris didn't drop her smile, but she knew she needed to drop the dickhead comments.

"We ain't hear nothin' 'bout it," the taller one remarked.

"Nah," Kris answered, "ya wouldn't have, because he just told me a few minutes ago. I was servin' him his food, and he asked me to come check. Told me to get back with him when I finished."

"The Prefect said that?" The short one's eyes were narrow, his voice skeptical. Kris knew why, of course. From everything she'd heard, the Prefect was basically stumbling around like a shell of himself.

He wasn't askin' nobody to do nothin'.

Yet, here Kris was with a lie she had to keep forcing.

"Sure did. If you want to go check with him, feel free. I'll wait here while you go ask the Prefect to repeat himself to a lowly sentry. Either of you mugs got a cig I can smoke while you're doin' it?"

The sentries looked at each other, then the big one shrugged and the little one grinned.

"Go on, soup girl. Try not to hurt yourself on the stairs."

Kris kept her mouth shut, although she wanted to say *something*.

She was getting what she wanted, though—and that was all that mattered.

Kris walked between the two guards and started up the spiraling stairs. She moved quickly and silently, but when the stairs kept going higher, she found herself short of breath.

There was a fuckin' *lot* of them.

Finally, though, Kris reached the top.

"Never again," she whispered, completely out of breath. "Brighten's right. I'm never doing this again."

Last time, this was where she and Brighten had stopped. Now, though, she had to go inside and find out what other information she could.

You've found out enough, she thought. *You know more now than anyone back at the shanty does. You don't need to go inside. Just turn around and head back down.*

Then why the hell did ya come up here? Get yer ass inside and quit bein' scared.

Whatever was going on in Sidnie, people weren't *dying.* She wasn't going to be killed here. She might get a few days in the stocks or something, but that was it.

"Death ain't on the other side of this door," she whispered, steeling herself.

On her last word, the door opened.

A man stood in front of her. He wore a sword and no smile.

"It just might be, little girl. How about you come in and find out?"

Kris tried to run; she turned, but the man was much too quick.

He grabbed her shirt and yanked her in the room.

"My name's Harold. Nice to meet you."

He slugged Kris in the face, and the world went dark.

Brighten was exhausted as he made his way across the city. The magic school had stretched late into the night, the mage apparently needing no sleep.

One kid had complained about the late hour, but that ended quickly when Rendal had him tossed out just like the first one.

There were no more complaints.

He and Kris had agreed to meet back at the shanty, so he didn't bother looking on the streets for her. She should have been back long before him. Making it to the tower was dangerous, but it was relatively quick.

He reached the shanty about four in the morning.

William sat inside, using a whetstone to sharpen his sword. Erin lay with her back to him, apparently asleep—though Brighten couldn't understand how anyone could sleep with that going on.

William looked up. "You two find anything?"

Brighten's eyes narrowed. "Where's Kris?"

"With you, ain't she?" William asked. He stopped sharpening his sword.

"No. We split up. I went into the magic school, and she went to the castle."

Erin started blinking, and Lucie came out of the back room.

Brighten had missed Verith on entering, but saw the man stand up from a cot.

"She ain't back yet." William stared at Brighten, his face unreadable. "Why did ya split up?"

"She should be here. She should have been here hours ago." Brighten's anxiety was quickly ramping up.

"She ain't, son. I been up all night waitin' for you two little ingrates. Nobody's come." William stood up. "When was the last time ya saw her?"

"Before I went to the damned magic school!" Brighten shouted, tears flooding his eyes.

Lucie walked quickly across the room and put her arms on him. "Hey, there, it's okay. That girl is as fast as anyone I've ever seen, 'cept maybe for my friend Riley. Ain't nobody got ahold of her."

Brighten shook his head. "No. She would be back by now. There's no way she's still at the castle, and there's no way she would have gone anywhere else."

William walked over, and his voice was calm when he spoke. "You say she should be back. You sure about that, son? I need to know the truth, not what fear is tellin' ya."

Brighten nodded. "Yes. There's no way she's not back."

William sighed and looked at Lucie. "You need to just start listenin' to me. That's the new rule: what William says goes. Understand?"

"That's what we need," Lucie remarked. "The dumbest among us making all decisions. I'd rather just walk to the castle and tell Rendal to kill me." She turned to Brighten and winked. "I'm still makin' decisions, and right now, I'm tellin' ya, William is going to go see what's what with Kris. He'll get her back if she's been taken, okay?"

"I'm only agreein' because that's exactly what I was about to tell the kid. The rule still stands—what I say goes." He gave Brighten a slight smirk, and some of the boy's worries dissipated.

The man was huge, and his confidence was catching.

"You need to toughen up, lad." The big man tightened his grip on Brighten's shoulder. "So you're comin' with me. And while you're at it, you're gonna tell me all about this little magic school."

"What are we going to do?" Brighten swallowed.

"I thought you were smarter than that, boy. If you say she went to the castle and didn't come out, where do you think we should look for her?" William asked.

"You're *not* smarter than you look," Brighten shot back. "There ain't no way you're getting in them gates. Her and I did because we have a hookup and because we're small and fast. Or at least *she* is. You go anywhere near that place and you'll be arrested. If you are who you say you are, they'll kill you."

William looked at Lucie. "This is your doin', ya know that? Ya got him thinkin' like a scared woman only a few days after meetin' him."

Lucie rolled her eyes but said nothing.

William looked at Verith. "You goin' or stayin'?"

"I'll stay in case something happens here. Two of us going won't do much."

"Smart man," William responded and looked at Brighten. "Time to grow a pair of balls, kid. Let's go get your friend back."

Rendal came back to the tower in good spirits. The first night of class had gone well, and he was beginning to organize what he would do with the teenagers.

Tomorrow the castle might hear from a few parents about their precious little ones being removed from the school, but Rendal was about to implement phase two of his plan.

Phase two meant no more complaints.

He'd start that tomorrow.

Rendal opened the door to the room at the top of the tower, walked in, and immediately stopped. "What is this?"

A young girl sat in front of him, an ugly bruise on the side of her face.

"We had some company while you were gone, sir," Harold answered. He stood behind the wet bar, a glass of whiskey untouched in front of him. He gestured to it.

Rendal crossed the room and took the drink. He kept his eyes on the girl, and she stared back.

He took a sip and asked Harold, "So, who is this?"

"I don't know her name, but she *is* stubborn. Won't say a word to me," Harold answered. "I thought about hurting her a bit more, but then figured I would just let you see her."

Rendal looked at Mason. "You know her?"

"If I did, would I tell *you*?" Mason spat back.

"No, probably not. You're a most unpleasant man, Mason. You should take life less seriously, especially given how close yours is to ending." Rendal looked at the girl, grinning. "You didn't feel like talking to Harold, huh?"

"The sonofabitch sucker-punched me when I walked in. Then says he wants to hurt me some more. Come do it now when I'm ready." The girl's eyes held hatred.

"A lively one, yes?" Rendal asked without looking away.

Harold didn't respond, and Rendal liked that. The man understood his place.

"I don't think you know her, Mason." Rendal took a step closer, holding his drink in his right hand. "You can hide nothing from me, dear. Not your name nor where you're from, or why you came here. To me, you are an open book."

"To me, you're an overgrown pubic hair." The girl didn't so much as flinch.

Rendal laughed. "Oh, I like her, Harold." He went into her mind. He had to admit he was growing tired, and he would need to recharge soon. The green bracelet was completely drained.

Still, he had enough energy to get inside the girl's head.

He saw everything within seconds.

"Kris. That's a pretty name."

"I wish I could say the same about you, but you look like a wrinkled nutsack." She glared at him, apparently not impressed with his brief bit of magic.

"They're here, Harold." Rendal didn't turn from looking at the girl.

"Who, sir? Riley?" Harold asked.

"Everyone but her and that mage, it seems," Rendal answered. "The rest of the crew came, but Riley didn't. Kris here doesn't know why she didn't come."

"Can you see where they are?"

Rendal nodded. "The poor part of the town. I believe Kris here thinks of it as Shantyville. Or, as she calls it, *fuckin'* Shantyville."

"Would you like me to go get them?" Harold asked.

"I'm considering that." He looked at Mason. "Where is she? Where's Riley?"

"You're dumber than you look, Rendal. How am *I* to know where she is? The only time I leave your presence is when you throw me into a cage." Mason glared at the mage.

"And if you're not careful with that mouth, you'll end up right back there. I *know* you haven't been around her, Mason. I'm asking you to use that poor excuse for a brain you've been given and *think*. Where else might she be?"

Rendal took a step closer.

Mason shrugged. "I have no idea. As far as I know, she would have come with them."

Rendal's hand flashed up and squeezed the air. Mason

grabbed his neck and his mouth sprang open as he started gasping for air.

"*Think*, Mason. *Think* as if your very life depends on it," Rendal growled.

"I…don't…know," Mason choked out.

Rendal dropped his hand, and Mason started coughing. He fell onto his side, taking deep, ragged breaths.

Rendal turned back around and looked at Harold. "This is most disconcerting."

Harold said nothing, but he was obviously frightened.

Because Rendal was angry. Riley was supposed to be here with the rest of them; *that* had been the plan.

He closed his eyes and listened to Mason coughing on the couch.

Rendal was exhausted, and he didn't have the energy to deal with all this right now. He needed to rest and recharge.

He shook his head. "No, I don't want you to go get them. They can't stop me, regardless of what they try. We're going to focus on this city. Riley will come, and when she does, I want everything ready."

He opened his eyes and faced Kris.

"I have a better idea."

"What's that, sir?" Harold asked.

"We'll set up bait for a few of them. Maybe they'll come looking for her and save us the trouble of going after them." Rendal felt his tiredness fade momentarily. "Tomorrow. Call the kingdom. We'll make it a public display."

"What the hell are you talkin' about?" Kris spat.

"You, my dear, are either going to bring us who we want or you're going to be in a lot of pain. Either way,

Sidnie is going to start moving down the route I have planned for it."

Rendal spoke to Harold next. "Go ahead and take her away. Drain her tonight, and tomorrow have her outside the castle. We'll do it at dusk."

"Don't you put your fuckin' hands anywhere near me." The girl's face was granite as she'd jumped to her feet.

Rendal laughed. "I do like this one. She has spunk. Would you like me to handle her, Harold, or do you think you can?"

"Oh, big men, the both of ya," Kris snapped. "Going to 'handle' a little girl. You don't know how bad you're fuckin' up right now."

"The mouth on her, Harold," Rendal joked. "Have you ever heard such a thing?"

"Poor parenting," Harold remarked with a slight smirk.

"William's gonna be both your daddies when he finds out what's happened to me. Go ahead and do what you want now, because once he gets here, it's lights out for the two of you." Kris put her hands up as if she were ready to fight.

"Oh, the hell with it," Rendal declared.

He flicked his fingers dismissively, and the girl flew against the wall. She hit it *hard*, knocking off picture frames.

The girl slid to the ground, her eyes blinking lazily. She sat like that for a minute and then fell to her left, unconscious.

Rendal turned to one of the other couches in the Prefect's office. "Drain her and get the setup ready for tomorrow."

"Yes, sir."

Harold didn't leave as Rendal sat down. "What else is there?"

"The Prefect's advisors. They're making noise. They're not buying what he's telling them," Harold answered.

Rendal looked at the Prefect. "Aw, hell, Harold. Did you see this?"

Slidell had pissed himself. He was standing in the corner, and a dark stain spread across his crotch.

"No, sir. I've been dealing with the brat."

"Well, get him fucking cleaned up too." Rendal was pissed. Problems everywhere he looked. "What about these damn advisors?"

"We're going to have to deal with them," Harold told the mage. "The Prefect… It's up to you, sir, whether he's going to be able to handle such a conversation."

The man stared blankly out at the room, not hearing them.

Rendal sighed. "He's *deep* in the hypnosis. It may be time to simply replace them."

"You?"

"No, Harold," Rendal sneered. "With Belarus. Just get these two out of here and leave me in peace."

"Yes, sir," Harold responded quickly.

He commanded the Prefect to follow him and threw the girl over his shoulder.

Mason slowly sat up on the couch. His throat was swollen and red.

"Mason, it's just you and me now," Rendal jested, lying down and stretching his legs out.

"Sounds like things are getting too big for you to handle, master mage."

"Sounds like you just need to listen a little closer," Rendal rebuked the Assistant Prefect. "Tomorrow the kingdom changes, and maybe your friends die, too."

William and Brighten stood in the crowd. William was massive, but he wore a hooded cloak that hung all the way to his feet. The boy practically disappeared in his wake.

No one was looking at the two of them. The world was focused on the stage up front.

It was empty as of yet, but the announcement had gone far and wide.

A traitor.

A spy.

Discovered within Sidnie's own people.

"That's her," William had remarked the moment he heard.

"She's no damn traitor!" Brighten had shouted.

"Calm yourself, boy," William responded. "I know she ain't a traitor, but that's what Rendal is gonna call her. That's what he's setting up with all this."

"What's gonna happen to her?" Brighten had asked.

"May kill her. May be setting us up," the big man concluded. "Can't say just yet."

The two had come to the front of the castle. A massive stage had been constructed, standing five feet above everyone.

Stocks had been set up in the middle of it.

"What's that mean?" Brighten whispered as the two slowly made their way through the crowd.

"Son, do I look like a damned mind reader?" William asked without looking down. The cloak mostly hid the broadsword on his back, but not completely.

"No, but have you seen anything like this before? What happens?"

William kept walking, not slowing. He needed to get closer to the stage if he were going to be able to stop anything.

"Usually, with a block like this in such a public place, it means beheading," he answered.

"Be-*whatting*?" The boy reached for William's arm, trying to pull him to a stop.

William growled but halted, then looked down.

"We can't let them hurt her," Brighten whispered sharply.

William wanted to keep moving forward. He wasn't good with this kind of stuff; he didn't have kids and didn't want them, but the boy was freaking out.

He squatted down, his massive frame coming even with Brighten.

"Why do you think we're here, kid? For our health? Did you need to walk to keep your heart in shape?"

Brighten shook his head and William grinned at him.

"Hell, no. Your heart is in tip-top shape, and my heart's the strongest thing in this damned kingdom. We're here because we're not gonna let anything happen to your smart-mouthed friend, all right?"

Brighten nodded, although he still looked scared.

"It's your job to keep your eyes peeled and your senses

alert," William continued. "You leave the fightin' to me. Ain't nobody in this kingdom going to hurt me, you, or her. Now get some steel in your spine and let's be heroes."

"Heroes?"

"Hell, yes. Heroes, kid. Whatcha think we're in this for?" William grinned. "Glory."

He stood up and started moving forward again.

A few minutes later, Sidnie's Prefect walked out onto the stage.

"Thank you…all for coming."

William chuckled. "Something's definitely wrong with that man."

No one in the crowd could think anything different. The man wasn't *quite* drooling on himself, but he looked close to it. His voice was almost disembodied, completely separate from the person speaking.

"That's not the Prefect," Brighten said.

"Whatcha mean?" William didn't look away from the stage. He hadn't taken his sword out but was ready the moment it needed to happen.

"I mean, it looks like him, but that's *not* the man everyone here knows. It's some kind of weird replacement." Brighten sounded like he was almost in awe of what he was seeing.

"That's the mage's work, boy. Be ready."

"I want…to introduce you…to my newest…advisor. He is head of…of…of…"

"The magic school!" another voice boomed from behind the stage.

William knew who it was. Fuckin' Rendal.

Sure enough, the mage walked onto the stage. "Thank you very much for that introduction, Prefect Slidell."

"You're…welcome," the Prefect forced out before shuffling off stage.

"I'd like to introduce myself and tell you all a bit more about the magic school you've all heard of. It's founding certainly wasn't decided on a whim. The Prefect definitely didn't *want* to shut down all the independent teachers, but there's been a serious development."

The mage's face grew grave.

"Your Prefect contacted me after discovering the development, and he was wise to do so. My name is Rendal Hemmons, and I'm a master mage in a way that even Prefect Slidell has not achieved. That's not a slight on your great leader, only the truth. That's why he brought me here."

The crowd grew quieter around William, and he thought he understood why. The mage was using his skills to transfer fear. The crowd *believed* him, even after only a few words.

"We've found a spy. A traitor to Sidnie."

Complete and total silence. If William took a single step forward, it would be noticed.

The mage continued, "Across the Badlands is a kingdom called New Perth. You've heard of it, no?"

"We know 'em!" someone shouted, real anger in his voice.

"They're the ones who flipped this person. This youthful person. I wanted to try to save her, to flip her back to Sidnie, but…it isn't possible."

The mage looked down at his feet.

"She's too far gone, and we imagine she's given an unfathomable amount of information to New Perth. She was caught *inside* the castle, and do you know what she was looking for?"

Rendal looked up.

"Blueprints. The plans to the very building that houses our Prefect and our nobles."

"*WHO?*" someone screamed. "*WHO DID IT?*"

"Would you like to see her?" the mage whispered, but the noise rolled across everyone as if he'd screamed it.

"*SHOW HER!*"

"*GIVE US THE TRAITOR!*"

"Bring her out," Rendal commanded.

William saw movement behind the stage, and someone tossed Kris out onto the wooden platform.

She looked at the crowd, ferocity in her eyes.

"This is her," the mage called out. "The traitor. The one who came to steal the blueprints and give them to the enemy!"

Rendal stepped forward, not looking at Kris.

"What should we do to her?"

"She's a traitor!" someone shouted.

"Put her in prison!"

"Kill her!"

William felt the boy pulling on his cloak. He looked down at him. "This isn't normal. People shouldn't be shouting like this. It's not how Sidnie works."

"I know." William nodded and looked back up. The mage was doing something to these citizens.

"There are *more* traitors, though," the mage declared. "Some are here with us now, right in this crowd."

"He knows," Brighten whispered.

William only shook his head, but he saw people looking around. At their friends, their family, their neighbors.

"Come forth, traitors, and we will save this girl's life. Otherwise, she'll be sentenced to death."

William kept his head high, staring right at Rendal. He didn't think the mage had spotted him yet.

He looked down at Brighten. "Ready to be heroes?"

The kid swallowed but nodded.

"Go around to the back of the stage. When it's time, I want you to run onto it, okay?" William asked.

"How will I know when it's time?"

William grinned. "Trust me, you'll know. Now go!"

The kid dashed off. William looked at the mage, still standing at the edge of the platform.

"Riley," William whispered to himself. "I'm gonna need you to learn this damned magic so I have some help over here."

He stepped forward, dropping his cloak and revealing the massive broadsword hanging on his back.

"Hey, Rendal!" he shouted. "I'm no traitor, but I'll save that girl all the same!"

Kris grinned as she turned to the mage. "I told you. You're fucked now."

CHAPTER FOURTEEN

R iley watched the queen walk farther out into the sand.

Worth sat to her left, his diminishing bag of wine between his legs.

Rachel and Thomas were to her right, both silent. Riley knew they didn't trust her or Worth, but she didn't care. They didn't matter. Only the queen—Alexandra—mattered.

Another day had passed, and Riley was dying to learn something, *anything*, but the queen had insisted they all rest yesterday. Now, they'd ventured out of the tunnels into the Badlands.

"The problem isn't you, Riley," Alexandra stated as she turned around. "It's what you've been taught."

"What do you mean?" Riley asked.

"What do you know about magic?" the queen responded.

Riley didn't hesitate. "It's dangerous. It can hurt people if it's not controlled, and most people can't control it."

"See?" Alexandra smiled.

Riley's brow furrowed. "I…"

"You didn't even realize you believed that so completely, did you?"

Riley shook her head.

"So, no wonder you can't activate your magic. You have a mental block against it, Riley. You've been taught it's dangerous. You're a good person, so why would you use it?"

Riley was dumbfounded.

"She stubborn," Worth interjected. "Very stubborn. Need better student!"

Riley looked over and saw Worth grinning. "Maybe I just needed a better teacher."

"Aye, Worth best teacher, betcha. Best in all the world. Brought you to underground people, didn't he?"

Riley glanced at the queen, knowing that he'd used a derogatory term.

She only rolled her eyes, then said, "Focus, Riley."

Riley nodded.

"To gain access to your magic, you'll have to break down the wall your mind's created. It's not your teachers. It's not your enemies. It's *you*."

"But how do I outwit my own mind?" Riley asked.

"You don't want to outwit your mind. You want to show it that it's been taught false things," Alexandra answered.

"I mean, I know that logically. I've seen Worth. I've seen William. Hell, I've seen *myself* use magic in good ways, but my mind isn't listening." Riley looked at Worth for agreement.

The tent man only stared out into the desert as if he hadn't heard anything she'd said.

"We're not talking about logic here." The queen took a step closer. "We're talking about *understanding*. We're really talking about faith."

Riley looked at her.

"I live beneath the ground in tunnels built by people long dead in the middle of a desert. I do it because I have *faith* that someone is coming to move the world forward." Alexandra smiled. "I fully understand how crazy that looks to the outside world. Thomas and Rachel know it looks crazy too. We don't care. We have faith."

She nodded at Riley.

"You have no faith in magic, only in your sword. You need *faith*."

"How do I get it?" Riley asked.

"Lie down," the queen commanded.

Riley looked down. "Here? In the sand?"

"If you see some water, you may lie in that instead," Alexandra offered. "I don't see any, though, so the sand might have to suffice."

She winked at Riley.

"You're as bad as Worth," Riley remarked. She sat down on the ground, then laid back so that she was staring at the cloudless sky. "Still not feeling any faith."

"See what Worth mean?" he called from the side. "She so stubborn."

"Worth, you keep it up, you're gonna feel my boot right in your ass." Riley grinned.

"Focus," the queen demanded. "Close your eyes."

Riley did.

"Now I want you to start thinking about the good things magic can give you," Alexandra directed. "See them, Riley. See them as if you're living them."

"Like what?" Riley didn't fully understand.

"What can magic give you right now that nothing else can?" the queen asked.

Riley closed her eyes.

What can *magic give me?* she wondered. *Why am I here? Why am I trying so hard to learn all this?*

The answers were simple.

Mason.

New Perth, the kingdom she loved.

"What can magic give you?" the queen asked. "See it, Riley. Let your mind *feel* it."

Riley went back to the compound, to the battle where Rendal *took* Mason.

She didn't focus on what actually happened, but on what she *wanted* to happen. Riley saw Rendal holding Mason, the mage's shoulder injured. Fire blazing from someone to her left.

But instead of coming for him with a blade, fire swept from Riley's hands. It moved in a blazing tornado, and it wrapped around the dark mage's legs, burning him.

He released Mason.

"That's good." The queen spoke softly. "But magic isn't just for vengeance, Riley. That's part of the same false beliefs you've been fed. Think about the good that can spring from it."

The good? Riley wondered.

New Perth. She went there. Mason was home. Worth was there with his remaining clan. William.

She saw kids playing in the street, but instead of toys rolling around on the ground, they were flying in the *air*.

Riley heard the kids' laughter.

She saw the head doctor standing over a sick person, but instead of his instruments, he used only his hands. He was healing them. With *magic*.

Riley saw William training future warriors. Flames and electricity flowed from their hands, their eyes red. They weren't angry, though. They were righteous fighters. They would only fight on the side of good.

"You see, Riley?" Alexandra whispered. "*Those* are things you want. *Those* are things that will help all of New Perth."

Riley nodded, still watching the images in her mind.

"But you can only have them if you believe in them. You can only use magic if you believe it'll bring good, not pain."

Riley's hands dug into the sand.

She saw herself kneeling in front of Mason, eyes red, ready to do his will. Her magic was *his* magic because she served him.

Her magic was *New Perth's* magic.

And wasn't that the point of all this?

"*YEEEEESSS!*"

Worth's shout broke Riley's concentration. She was rising to her feet, her eyes open and her sword free of its sheath before she realized what was happening.

Worth was dancing around, shaking his hands at the sky.

Riley spun to Alexandra.

The queen was smiling, but Riley didn't understand.

"Is it her?" Thomas asked from behind. Riley had

forgotten he and Rachel were there. She turned to them, and that was when she finally saw.

A circle of fire burned around her feet. She hadn't seen it because she'd been focused on Worth's scream.

It encircled her, the flames reaching as high as her ankles.

"I'm not doing that," Riley whispered.

"You magic!" Worth shouted at her.

"If not you, then who?" the queen asked.

Riley glanced at her. "You. Them. I don't know, but it's not me."

"Are any of our eyes red, Riley?" Alexandra responded. "Because yours are."

Riley looked down at the flames.

"They haven't gone out, and you're not in any danger." The queen stepped a bit closer. "Go on. You can control them."

Riley realized she could. She realized that the fire she saw at her feet was the same as her sword—something she would control as its master.

She squatted down and gently placed a finger above a single flame. It reached up and licked her skin but didn't burn her.

She raised her hand six inches and the flame grew with it.

Riley grinned. "I did that."

"Yes, you did," Alexandra answered.

Riley put both palms over the fire.

She held them there for a second, then rose to her full height in a graceful spin, her hands sweeping around the circle of fire.

It exploded upward, surrounding her completely and shooting into the sky like a geyser.

"Oh! Oh!" Worth shouted. "Look!"

Riley stepped into the fire. It moved around her body like water, causing her no pain at all.

The Right Hand grinned as she spoke. "It's time to go to Sidnie. It's time to kick that mage's ass."

FINIS

Whew! You made it to the end! Have a beer (or wine, as Worth would urge)!

As a writer, I never truly know where my characters are going to end up. They take on their own lives and more or less direct me. I know that may sound kind of pretentious, but it's the truth. Watching Riley evolve during this book was breathtaking for me. I knew she would end up being able to use her magic, but I didn't know *how* she would get there.

I'm glad she finally made it. It's going to make her ass-kicking ability that much better.

As this book progressed, I really started hating Rendal more and more. His desire for power and his willingness to do *anything* to turn Riley… I'm looking forward to the day when he gets his comeuppance.

I'd like to thank Michael again for giving me the opportunity to write in his world. It's a fascinating set of parameters he's set up and I'm truly enjoying building off it.

I can see this series stretching on for quite a few more

books. Riley is just now learning her powers, but is that going to be enough to attack Rendal? Or is it going to take her training longer and harder? But will she even be *able* to wait that long?

Okay, enough of me pontificating. I'm going to get back to the salt mines and start writing some more. See you in book 3!

All the best,
Jace

THANK YOU for not only reading this story but these *Author Notes* as well.

(I think I've been good with always opening with "thank you." If not, I need to edit the other *Author Notes*!)

RANDOM (*sometimes*) THOUGHTS?

Seriously Jace?

You are starting to hate Rendal more and more?

I need to pay more attention to where you live and come have a heart to heart about a certain someone's death.

Hmmmm.

Well, that seems kinda murder-minded of myself, doesn't it? Like I'm a serial killer let loose to discuss the death of someone who could just be misunderstood, right?

Hell no, off with their head!

And now, a picture of white bunnies so Michael has a moment to collect his thoughts.

HOW TO MARKET FOR BOOKS YOU LOVE

We are able to support our efforts with you reading our books, and we appreciate you doing this!

If you enjoyed this or ANY book by any author, especially Indie-published, we always appreciate if you make the time to review a book, since it lets other readers who might be on the fence to take a chance on it as well.

AROUND THE WORLD IN 80 DAYS

One of the interesting (at least to me) aspects of my life is the ability to work from anywhere and at any time. In the future, I hope to re-read my own *Author Notes* and remember my life as a diary entry.

Dec 18th, 2018

So, I am sitting in the restaurant at the Trophy Club Country Club … club. (Seems redundant.)

I am at one of the booths that I used to write at when I was just starting out, looking out over the golfers and golf range down below. The grass is all brown for us those of us here in Texas (most don't seed their homes with winter rye) and it's just a degree or four too cold for me to sit outside to eat.

This might be the last time I ever visit this location, as (I hope) we get the house here in Texas sold. I'm a little melancholy about the whole experience, and while I don't think (when I'm in Vegas) that I want to come back and visit, it feels like putting on a comfortable set of gloves when I'm here.

I've got about twenty items I'm late with at the moment, with all of the time working with contractors and stuff, so I'm going to drop off.

Before I do, thank you once again for making this job of creating stories so damned wonderful. I hope you (whatever day(s) you are reading this) have a wonderful week, weekend and a fantastic life.

And that we kill that SOB from up above.

FAN PRICING

If you would like to find out what LMBPN is doing and the books we will be publishing, just sign up at http://lmbpn.com/email/. When you sign up, we notify you of books coming out for the week, any new posts of interest in the books and pop culture arena, and the fan pricing on Saturday.

Ad Aeternitatem,

Michael Anderle

OTHER AGE OF MAGIC BOOKS

THE RISE OF MAGIC

with CM Raymond and LE Barbant

Restriction (1) – Reawakening (2) – Rebellion (3) – Revolution (4) – Unlawful Passage (5) – Darkness Rises (6) – The Gods Beneath (7) – Reborn (8)

STORMS OF MAGIC

with PT Hylton

Storm Raiders (1) – Storm Callers (2) – Storm Breakers (3) – Storm Warrior (4)

TALES OF THE FEISTY DRUID

with Candy Crum

The Arcadian Druid (1) – The Undying Illusionist (2) – The Frozen Wasteland (3) – The Deceiver (4) – The Lost (5) – The Damned (6) – Into The Maelstrom (7)

A NEW DAWN

with Amy Hopkins

Dawn of Destiny (1) – Dawn of Darkness (2) – Dawn of Deliverance (3) – Dawn of Days (4) – Broken Skies (5) – Broken Bones (6)

TALES OF THE WELLSPRING KNIGHT

with P.J. Cherubino

Knight's Creed (1) – Knight's Struggle (2) – Knight's Justice (3) - Etheric Knight (4)

THE HIDDEN MAGIC CHRONICLES

with Justin Sloan

Shades of Light (1) – Shades of Dark (2) – Shades of Glory (3) – Shades of Justice (4)

PATH OF HEROES

with Brandon Barr

Rogue Mage (1)

HAND OF JUSTICE

with Jace Mitchell

The Dark Mage (1) - Chasing Madness (2)

BOOKS BY MICHAEL ANDERLE

For a complete list of books by Michael Anderle, please visit:

www.lmbpn.com/ma-books/

All LMBPN Audiobooks are Available at Audible.com and iTunes

To see all LMBPN audiobooks, including those written by
Michael Anderle please visit:

www.lmbpn.com/audible